Director's Cut

Director's Cut

Jennifer Joyce Holland

SCORPIO PUBLISHING LLC   PORTLAND, OREGON

First Edition

Cover designs © 2009

John Roscoe Bischoff

jarknorse@hotmail.com

Scorpio Publishing LLC

623 SW Park Avenue

Portland, OR 97205

http://scorpiopublishing.us

LIBRARY OF CONGRESS CATALOGING-IN-PUBLICATION DATA

2009903785

ISBN 978-0-578-02071-6

Printed in the United States

To all of you — alive or dead — who helped me write this book.
I hope you know who you are.

PROLOGUE

What a long, strange trip it's been...
Grateful Dead

Tuck knew he was falling to his death, and as he fell, he marveled at what sped through his mind in its closing seconds. For one thing, he felt weightless in the damp air; he could see her tumbling, too, not far from him, her eyes closed, as if she were dead already. His heart broke, seeing her like that. And he thought, *This is it. It's just like they say in books.* For flashes of his life — correction, of his many lives — lit his mind at lightning's speed. He saw the movie theater, the English village, the French chateau, the Irish farmhouse, the monastery, the town square; the Saudi desert, his home town; he saw his wife, his sister, his child, his lover, his friends, the goat, the rope. He saw it all, every minute of it, uncut, no holds barred. Every minute of his life was thrown into stark relief against the dark shadow of a mountain that formed the backdrop to his life's final film. So quickly did it show, he hadn't time to wince at his less-than-kind actions, or to be embarrassed, or to rejoice.

His crash to earth forced this final word from his lips: *Zia.*

1

Foyer

There are more things in heaven and earth, Horatio
Than are dreamt of in your philosophy.
Shakespeare, *Hamlet*

Catching a glimpse of herself in the old movie theater's mirrored wall, Tuck's wife dimpled briefly, and then minced her way down the hall to the ladies' room. Tuck couldn't help himself; he watched her, frankly admiring her swively hips and her thick, long black hair, the two assets that had snagged his attention twenty-five years ago. She was still beautiful, even after a quarter-century of marriage and bearing three children. *Too bad she's such a bitch.* Tuck sighed and decided to get some popcorn while he waited for her return.

Strolling over to the refreshment stand, he waited behind two lesbians who couldn't decide whether to have Milk Duds or Raisinets. *Jesus, pick the Milk Duds already. We've got a show to go to here.* When it was his turn, he told the toothy kid with the pockmarked face who stood behind the counter, "Large popcorn, extra butter." He hesitated. "No. Wait. Better just make that two Cokes: one Diet, one regular." *The wife hates popcorn. Gets her hands all greasy. Hates the smell of it on me.* Tuck sighed, and Toothy, hearing it, glanced over at him. Tuck flashed him a rueful smile as an apology. To himself he thought, *Damn, but it's my wedding anniversary, too. I should be able to order what I want at the movies at least one day a year.* He shrugged his shoulders. *Someday I'll have the balls to deal with her, but today's not the day.*

"Here you go, *fir.* Two Diet Coke*f.*" Toothy's freckled, acne-covered face creased into a wide smile.

Tuck stopped himself from saying, *What?!* Poor Toothy's "s" sounded like an "f." *It's a wonder anyone can understand him.. Anybody with teeth that big'd have trouble saying anything clearly.*

As if to prove Tuck right, Toothy continued, "*Vhat'll vee five buckf.*" Another smile from Toothy.

Tuck caught himself before he said *Fanks* to the kid. *Would ya look at that face. It's like a pizza. Jesus, if that's what working here has done to him, he should sue his boss. Toothy'll never get laid.* Tuck fished some money from his wallet and muttered a thank you, stuffing the wallet back into the pocket of his expensive jeans before taking the two Cokes from the counter.

"Oh, which one is the Diet?" he asked.

Toothy's smile faded. "*Vey're bof diet, fir.*" Toothy's crestfallen look touched Tuck in spite of himself. He gave Toothy the smile he often used on those he considered less intelligent or annoying, but harmless.

"No problem, kid. Diet's probably better for me anyway." To himself he added, *I hate Diet Coke. And I'm not trying to lose weight. Look at me! Do I look like I need to lose weight?* He flashed another quick semi-smile to Toothy, as if to make up for his less-than-charitable thoughts a moment earlier, then took the two Cokes and walked toward the middle of the mirrored foyer. He stood there, sipping the Diet Coke, wishing it were a beer instead.

My god, but that woman takes forever in the bathroom. Standing in the theater, waiting, he studied it as if seeing it for the first time. *Look at this room. I love those old wood banisters. I even love the cheesy crimson-velvet-flocked wallpaper. Reminds me of New Orleans, or maybe Toulouse.* His gaze shifted to the now-locked doors that had led to the opera box seats. A half-smile flickered across his lips. *I remember going up to those balcony seats in high school. Could really make out in the dark there. Got caught once—hell, more than once! What was that blonde's name? God, but she had great tits. The look on that usher's face! Jealous of me.* Tuck took a sip of the Coke and grimaced, quickly checking to see if anyone had seen him make a face. Tuck realized he was alone in the foyer; it was eerily quiet. *Damn, the movie must have started. Where is that woman?*

He started toward the hall to the restrooms, intending to tell his wife to get her ass out of there because the movie had started. He took a few steps in what he thought was the right direction, but the hall wasn't. *How'd I get turned around?* He pivoted slowly, searching for the hallway, certain he must have misremembered where it was, but it had simply vanished. He was still in the theater's foyer as such, but it was just a big, round room—and he was alone in it. There was no one behind the refreshment counter; there was no one in the ticket booth. It was spooky. *What was in that Coke?* Tuck thought he might be hallucinating.

"What the fuck's happening here?" His shout echoed a little, bounding off the flocked wallpaper. He caught a movement out of the corner of his eye, and he whirled around. Nothing; no one. He glanced up and was startled to see large screens, like big plasma television sets, suspended from the ceiling. They hung next to each other along the coving that decorated the upper third of the room. His jaw dropped open at the sight of them. He felt something drop from his mouth to the floor, and he looked down. A saliva-coated kernel of popcorn had fallen on the red carpet. *Where did that come from?* Quickly, he looked at his right hand, which had, until a moment ago, held a Diet Coke. Both Cokes had disappeared: instead, he held a tub of buttered popcorn in his right hand, and nothing in his left.

With no one there to verify his sanity for him, he found himself gazing at the screens again—and there he was. He could see himself, pale and shocked, mouth open in a wide "O," holding the popcorn, and shaking his head slowly back and forth in disbelief. Turning carefully, he stared at each screen in turn.

Finally, tentatively, he waved with his free hand; the man on the screen waved, too. He set the popcorn on the floor as if it were a gun, watching himself on the screen the entire time. *Put the food down, son, nice and easy. Now back away.* He followed his own advice and retreated a few steps; then he ran back. The screen man did the same. He did a couple of jumping jacks, and then a little dance move. Mesmerized, he watched his screen self do it all. There was no doubt. *Yep, that's me up there.*

A new thought struck him, one that panicked him a bit. *I wonder if anyone else can see me?* Feeling stupid, Tuck picked up the tub and grabbed a handful of popcorn, shoving it into his mouth and chewing violently, as if the action would bring him back to normality. *Mmm. This popcorn's perfect. Extra butter, the real thing, not that fake crap you get sometimes.* He absent-mindedly wiped his fingers on his thigh, leaving greasy trails on the light denim. Glancing up, he could see the marks clearly. *God, she is going to kill me when she sees these grease marks. Better not even put these jeans in the laundry basket. I'll just throw 'em away and get some new ones. Of course, she'll bitch about that, too. I can't win. That woman bitches about everything I do.*

Discouraged, he went over to the refreshment counter, standing on his tiptoes and leaning over in an attempt to see if Toothy or the other employees were hiding from him. *Maybe this is how they get their kicks. Lord knows they have a boring enough job.* As expected, though, no one lurked under the counter.

He backed away slightly, cupping his hands around his mouth, sing-songing, "Come out, come out, wherever you are!" All he heard was a smoky-timbred echo, one that betrayed by its quaver the fear rising in him. He cleared his throat, feeling first one of his shirt pockets and then the other for the packet of mixed weed and tobacco he usually carried. *Shit. I left it with my climbing gear. Figured she'd never look there. She still thinks I quit smoking. Shit, shit, shit! I could really use a smoke.*

He went back to the stand again, wishing fervently for the old days, when movie theaters kept cigarettes in stock. *If nothing else, I can eat—as long as the candy and popcorn didn't disappear along with the employees, that is.* He eyed the big popcorn popper; it was still filled. The butter still bubbled gently in its own tureen. *I think I'll just help myself here.* His glance shifted to the closed cash register. *Bet there's no way to get the money out of that till. They sure wouldn't have given Toothy a key.* A thought struck him. *I could jimmy that till open!* He was just about to leap over the counter and try opening it, when the reflection of his movements caused him to look up. He saw himself on each screen, eight accusing plasma fingers, pointing at him. He hung his head, ashamed of himself for even thinking of trying to steal the money.

His head snapped back up a moment later. "But I am going to eat that popcorn if I'm trapped in here for too long," he said defiantly. "This might be some kind of weird test or joke or something, but if I get hungry, that's it. I'll eat it all, and I won't pay for it, either." *Man, I'm hungry* now. *Shouldn't have started talking about food.* The "surf 'n' turf" anniversary dinner he'd forced down (it was hard to enjoy a meal with his wife sitting there) now seemed hours and hours ago.

What time is it, anyway? He looked around for a clock, for he never wore a watch. He felt his upper left pocket for his cell phone. *Damn! Did I leave it in the restaurant?* He tried to remember where he'd last seen it. *No, I'm sure I brought it.* He looked up at a screen.

"Well, don't just stare! Do something useful, like tell me what time it is!" he yelled, now more pissed off than frightened.

Angry, he looked around for a wall clock. He was certain he had seen one earlier, but then again, nothing was as it seemed any more. In his growing rage, he failed to notice that every screen now told the time. Turning again to the counter, he caught the screens' reflections in one of the wall's mirrored tiles. The screens *had* changed. Astonished, he looked up and read it out loud: "0…2…0…6…." *I've been here six hours already? That can't be right.*

"Uh, thanks, but that doesn't help much. I know I haven't been here six hours." Puzzled, he rubbed his stubbly chin, shaking his head from side to side. Softly, he said, "God, I'm an idiot. I'm talking to a TV." *Say, maybe it's another time zone. I wish I knew which one it was. Hey! Maybe the screens are voice-activated—*

Before he had a chance to try his theory, "GMT" appeared on every screen, so each now read: "GMT 02:06." He tried to whisper "thank you," but what emerged from his lips was a sort of squeak. He cleared his throat and tried again. "Hey, GMT, that's pretty cool. That's what I'll call you: 'GMT.' That okay with you?" He felt better knowing the time, and his anger dissipated. He felt almost jaunty. "Can you do any other tricks, GMT?" He thought for a moment, letting his imagination run wild. "Could you rustle up some weed and a six-pack?" He chuckled wistfully. *Wouldn't it be great if it really could? It'd be like having my own genie.*

Because he didn't expect the screen to answer, let alone provide him with drugs, he didn't look behind him until he heard a slight scraping sound from the direction of the counter. There, next to the popcorn machine, sat a six-pack of Budweiser and some still-yellow dandelions. *Oh, man, I'm losing it. This can't be happening.* He walked over and felt one of the cans. It was warm. He picked up the bunch of wilted dandelions. *They feel real.* He set the weeds down again. *I wish the beer was cold. Still, I should probably say thank you or something. I don't wanna be ungrateful.*

Clearing his throat, he managed to say, "Nice idea, very funny with the weeds. I like a good pun; nothing like a good pun..." His voice trailed off. *I'm talking to a TV. There's no one else here. Say what you mean, Tuck!* "Uh, I don't want to complain, but cold beer would have been better—maybe Sierra Nevada Pale Ale? I'm not too fond of Bud." *I hate it. Why bother drinking if it's gonna be Bud?* He picked up one of the dandelions, twirling its stem between his thumb and middle finger, pulling off its yellow petals one by one, in what he hoped was a nonchalant manner. "Oh, and just for the record, GMT, I'm using "weed" in the sense of ganja, marijuana, wacky-backy; that sort of weed. But thanks anyway." He sighed. "Great pun," he added.

He looked at each screen in turn and made a small bow. "Thank you... thank you... thank you... thank you... thank you... thank you... thank you... thank you."

Dizzy, he put his hand on the counter to steady himself. It knocked against something cold. He jumped back as if he'd received an electric shock.

"Holy shit!"

There was a cold six-pack of Sierra Nevada Pale Ale, and a bag of what he sincerely hoped was weed on the counter. He opened the bag and sniffed. "Jee-sus. This stuff is primo, GMT." He grinned slyly, folding his arms across his chest as he turned and looked boldly up at one of the screens.

"Any chance of some paper and a light?" He was starting to enjoy himself. He waited a moment, then glanced over his left shoulder. On the countertop was a newspaper and a flashlight.

"Haven't lost your sense of humor, I see." He paused. "Say, as long as you're at it, I'd like to do the crossword, so send a pencil. Let's see. . ." *What else should I get here? One packet—no, better make it three—Rizlas. Who knows how long I'll be able to ask for this stuff? Two ciggie lighters—hey! How 'bout green ones? No; red. A coupla pencils—sharpened! Key to the cash register, of course—*

Engrossed as he was making his mental list, Tuck forgot to watch the countertop, where each thing was arriving (or disappearing) as quickly as he thought of it. The sound of the key clinking on the counter, however, brought him back to reality, and he whirled around. Everything was there, exactly as he had ordered it.

Tuck gave a low whistle of admiration. His voice trembled as he spoke. "I've got to hand it to you, GMT. You really listened. I got everything I asked for." He reached for a cold beer and popped off its cap. He toasted, "Cheers, GMT," half-expecting it to cheer him back. But the screen remained silent and dark, except for the time display: "GMT 02:24." *I've always said I wanted alone time. Guess that's what I'm getting now.* He felt the familiar pangs of loneliness creep into his chest. He didn't want his wife there, of course, but maybe his lover, or his kids. Even Toothy.

"So it's just you and me, GMT? I mean, it's a great trick with the beer and…stuff…" He stared at the pile on the counter, and realized how pitiful it would look to someone else—hell, it looked pitiful to him! *is this all he really wanted…*"but how long will this go on?" He sat down cross-legged on the floor, resigned. Absent-mindedly, he guzzled some beer, and then rolled a joint. As he lit it, he stole a peep over his shoulder—*force of habit, don't need to look, no one's watching me*—and then up at the screen. "No one's watchin' but you, right, GMT?" He sniffed the joint appreciatively. *This is good shit. Better not rush it.* He sat on the foyer floor enjoying the smoke.

He closed his eyes, and his mind drifted. He saw a mountain, a huge, solitary mountain, snow-capped. The sun shone high in the sky, beating down upon him as he stood on a large outcropping of stone. No, it was more of a mesa, wide and round. A stream burbled nearby, beckoning him. It would feel so cool on his hot skin. He would just float on that stream, that's what he would do…

"Tuck!"

He started at the sound of his name—spoken in a low, urgent voice— but not a soul appeared before his now wide-open eyes. *Must be stoned. This soon? Can't be. But I'm hearing things and I feel like philosophizing.*

"So, GMT," he heard himself slur, his voice sounding disembodied, far away. "What happened to the doors and hallway and stuff? And the people? like the employees and my wife and...and...the people, you know? And I mean...why me? That's the big question here, and I'd appreciate your feedback on that." He licked his lips, which felt a bit dry. "Thank you so much...'and have a pleasant tomorrow.'" He giggled.

Tuck took a nice, long toke, closing his eyes again, feeling the smoke reach like tiny fingers and massage each alveolus gently. He coughed a little and opened his eyes. The screens—gone! To his left he saw a door—the one to the theater—standing open. He squinched his eyes shut tight, and then opened them again. *Yep, still there.*

"Woo-hoo!" He jumped to his feet, remembering to cram the bag of weed and the lighters into his pocket. As he bent to pick up the popcorn tub and what was left of the beer, his cell phone dropped out of his jacket. Quickly he glanced over each shoulder, then looked up. Still no people; still no screens. But there was an open door. He didn't walk, he *ran* through it into the darkened theater.

2

Theater

Nothing will come of nothing: speak again.
Shakespeare, *King Lear*

This is more like it. Tuck let his breathing slow down, noticing that—at last—he could see other people, although none of them looked around when he came in. *Good thing, too. I want one of them beers while I'm here.* He hadn't had time to hide the six-pack under his jacket before racing in. It struck him as odd that no one heard him enter. Squinting in the dark, Tuck assessed the profiles of those he saw, trying to find a familiar one. Tuck knew just about everyone in his small town, but so far, he didn't recognize anyone he knew. He found a vacant seat two rows from the back, about eight in, no one in front of him, no one behind. *This way I won't have to worry about anyone seeing the beer. I might even be able to smoke.* He cheered at the thought; then he thought again. *Well, no. That'll never happen. Get real, Tuck.*

He settled in, placing a bottle in every cup holder within reach, but not until he'd opened it first. He hid each beer under his jacket to muffle the noise, and then coughed as he popped off each cap. When he finished his clandestine beer openings, he took the nearest bottle and drank deeply from it. *Perfect. This is the life.* He stuffed popcorn in his mouth, and a tiny stream of butter trickled its way down his chin, losing itself in his five-o'clock shadow. He just about wiped it off with the back of his hand. Instead, boldly, he left the dribble there. *She can't see me. No one can see me. I say,* the butter stays! He chuckled—a short, gravelly, dry sound that stayed mostly way back in his throat.

Whether from the effects of the beer or the pot, he was enjoying himself to the extent that he didn't notice how quiet the theater was. No one had turned around; no one was talking; the screen was dark. No trailers played; no commercials danced across the screen. Instead, it was dark, blank, soundless, lifeless. Only a wan light came from the doorway through which Tuck had walked, and another glimmered from under a door at the farthest end of the theater, on the opposite wall, near the screen.

Now that Tuck was comfortable, he surveyed the seats before him more closely, confident in his anonymity. He tried again to make out, in the dimness, who was sitting nearby. *Is that Gerry's wife up there?* He peered at the back of a blonde head about eight rows ahead and to the left of him. *You'd think she'd wash her hair once in a while.* He shuddered when he remembered her greasy, lank hair. *Pretty chubby, but a nice lady. Bought that chainsaw for Gerry that one year. True love, buying your man a chainsaw.* He looked to his right. *Shit. That looks like my brother. Who's he with this time? She looks like a slut from where I'm sitting.* He tried focusing his eyes into a really good stare, squeezing them nearly shut in the process, refusing to put on the distance glasses the doctor had prescribed for him. *Nah. That's not him. I don't know who she is, either. How come there are so many strangers here?* He drank some more, smacking his lips afterward. *Probably a crappy movie. Shoulda read the reviews. What's it called, anyway? Probably some chick flick* SHE *wanted to see.* The thought of his wife first flickered, then went out. He concentrated more on the beer he held, which he finished in one long swig.

He drew another beer from a nearby cup holder, carefully placing the empty one into the cardboard carrier so he could recycle it later. He sat back, the beer in his left hand, the tub of popcorn between his legs. He took a meditative swig, then a handful of kernels. His gaze shifted to the screen, and his beer hand stopped mid-raise. He could see himself, bigger than life, with a look of incomprehension on his face magnified for all to see. Also featured prominently was the bottle of Sierra Nevada. *Oh shit.* He quickly tried to hide the bottle, dropping it in the process. He smoothed back his longish brown-going-gray hair with his greasy fingers, and tried to wipe the butter, now congealed, from his chin. He furtively glanced around him to make sure the other bottles weren't visible, and then sat up straight, like he was in church. He tried a nonchalant look; it came across as a grimace. *I look like a kid who's just wet himself.* He attempted throwing his right arm casually over the back of the seat next to him and looking sideways. Ever so carefully, he used his peripheral vision and discovered that he was still the focus of the screen's attention. *Now I just look guilty as hell. Which I am, I suppose. I think I'd better explain myself.*

He cleared his throat. "Sorry, everyone. It's been a rough day, weird stuff happening." His voice sounded strained, strange even to his own ears. "We can all just watch the movie now, right?" He coughed slightly. "Anyone know what it's called, by the way?"

In unison, the heads of those in the audience turned in his direction; some were smiling. *That* is *Gerry's wife. I knew it.* Some were not. Although disconcerting in the extreme, having everyone stare at him, he was relieved to notice that no one seemed angry. It dawned on Tuck what kind of look he *was* getting, though. *They're expecting me to do something.*

"I don't know what you're expecting here, folks, but I just came here to watch a movie." *That got a reaction, though not the one I'd expected.* Most of them smiled and nodded knowingly, although some looked as confused as Tuck.

"I'd really feel better if you'd all quit looking at me, okay? I don't like being the center of attention." *Hmm. Looks of surprise cross the faces of those in the audience. I wonder why.* "Uh, there's nothing I can do for you." *That last part didn't sound too nice.*

Immediately, he sensed a change in atmosphere: from helpful and warm, to... Sad. *What did I say to make them sad? What did I say?* Each head but Tuck's turned toward the screen, and then, gradually, Tuck watched each person fade away. Within a minute, he was alone in the darkness. There was only himself, the real Tuck, and his magnified screen image, frightened, and with a glistening face.

"Wait! Wait! What did I say? Don't leave me here! Don't leave me!"

For the first time since this strange night had begun, Tuck let out the panic that had been building in him.

"N-o-o-o-o-o... n-o-o-o-o-o... n-o-o-o-o-o!"

The crimson-velvet-flocked theater walls absorbed, somewhat, his anguished voice.

And for the first time in his life, Tuck sobbed.

†

I just let Tuck cry. His sobs tore at my very soul, but there was nothing I could do until I became real for him, until he turned around, saw me, and asked for help. My job as recorder requires that I exercise no judgment or interference. I cannot do anything until I'm asked. Even then, there is only so much I can do.

It was hard to watch him fumble for non-existent tissues, and eventually deciding to blow his nose on his jacket sleeve. I nearly laughed when I saw him stare long and hard at the beer, as if he wasn't sure if it was the cause or the cure for his situation. That beer must have been pretty warm by now; people here lose their sense of time. He loved Sierra Nevada Pale Ale so much that one of the local bars got it in just for him. We used to share a bottle or two, sitting on my tiny deck in the soft summer sunsets, at the time we—briefly—crossed the line from friends to lovers. They seemed so long ago, those happy days, sitting in smiling silence.

At last, my presence reached the borders of Tuck's consciousness: he turned so quickly that some of the beer spilled from the bottle, and some popcorn ended up on the floor.

"Jesus! Zia! Where did you come from?" I enjoyed watching his eyes shift from terrified, to surprised, to relieved—all in about three seconds. A huge smile lit his face, and he vaulted over the theater seat, knocking what was left of the popcorn onto the floor.

He pumped my hand up and down, grabbing it in both of his. "I've never been so happy to see anyone in my whole life."

"Sure, you say that *now*...." My smile beamed back at him, too. "What do you think of the movie so far?"

"What fuckin' movie? If there was a movie, I must've missed it, because I've seen no movie. This has been the weirdest night of my life, Zia, bar none. I tell ya—" He stopped, lost for words. Then he hesitated. I could see him starting to put two and two together, and realizing that I may have witnessed his emotional outburst. (He was a smart man. His intelligence had attracted me to him in the first place. Okay—plus his gorgeous little butt and that sexy voice of his.)

"Zia, were you here when…uh…Have you been here long?" His voice cracked a little in that endearing way he has when his emotions slip past his usual intransigence.

"You might say I've always been here for you, Tuck." I raised my eyebrows suggestively and gave him that look that used to drive him wild. It didn't work; he was too mystified by the night's events to catch the innuendo. "But I don't think you want me to get all metaphysical on you. Don't worry, I'm no angel. Nor am I a figment of your imagination. Nor am I a judge. I guess I'm what I've always been: your friend, a writer, a recorder, an historian.

"You mean "*a* historian." He laughed. "Game on, Zia!"

"Yes. Yes; the game, my dear Tuck, is most certainly on, even if it looks more like a movie." Seeing his perplexed look, I gave him a brief hug, relishing his outdoorsy, manly smell. How I missed him! "The nice thing is, Tuck, I think we're *both* going to win this one." I ignored his puzzlement and caught hold of his hand, tugging him toward the aisle. "Come on. Grab those last two beers and let me show you something. And you can ask me any questions you'd like—can't promise I'll be able to answer them, though. I'm pretty new to this gig myself."

Dropping his hand, I collected my notebook and pen, and moved sideways toward the aisle, my long skirt catching on the seats' rough edges. Tuck handed me a beer when I reached him. I took a swig.

"Unh. Just a tad warm, my friend." I saw his semi-hurt look; he blamed himself for the warm beer. Realizing I'd sounded ungrateful, I added, "But it's wet, and it's free, so I'm going to enjoy it."

Tuck stared at me long and hard, his eyes squinting somewhat, the way he does when he's trying to solve a puzzle. I knew he wanted to ask questions, but he was neither sure which ones to ask, nor entirely sure he wanted to hear the answers. His quick brain was working near capacity. After a moment more, he spoke.

"Until I saw you, Zia, I thought I might be dead. Seeing you here makes me think I'm not. It could be a dream, because I know you used to have those kinds of dreams, "lucid," I think they were—but if so, what am *I* doing in it? Everything about me (here he touched, in turn, his head, his chest, his thighs) feels real, but the things that have happened—like food and weed and shit, appearing out of nowhere—*can't happen in real life.*" He paused to catch his breath. "Or are you here to tell me that they can? And if you are, how did *you* get here? Why didn't I see you before?"

"Geez, Tuck, I wish you had asked me *hard* questions." A little humor usually helped lighten things up a tad, but it wasn't working now. I'd never seen him look so unsure of himself.

"Seriously, Zia, how'd you get here? Did you walk into the movie theater, thinking you were just another schmuck coming to watch a show, and then have everybody disappear on you, and then have a bunch of TV sets give you free popcorn and beer and whatever you asked for? Did you feel like stealing? Did you have the same experience?" He was shouting now, his words tumbling over each other in their haste to escape.

This time I really had to laugh out loud. "No, no! Nothing like that at *all*. Are you making this up? You sound like a crazy man, Tuck!"

Embarrassment flickered in his eyes, and I instantly regretted what I had said. I knew from my own experience how finding myself in this theater, even though it had been under entirely different circumstances, had made me doubt my sanity. It was my turn to feel ashamed.

"I'm sorry, Tuck. Please forgive me." I used my gentlest voice. "You're not crazy at all—in fact, I'm starting to think we might represent the sanest folks on earth." His embarrassed look had been replaced by one of skepticism, Tuck's usual mode. I continued briskly, raising my voice a few notches, "My experience was completely different. I was reading Joyce's *Ulysses*, the "Penelope" section, and I kind of went into a daydream, marveling over Joyce's insanely beautiful writing ability." I saw him start at the word *insanely*. "Oh, geez, Tuck, I'm sorry! I didn't mean to use the "i" word, honest." He raised one eyebrow at me. "But you have to admit Joyce's writing style is a bit out there. Anywho, next thing I knew, I was here in this theater, right where you found me, with my notebook and pen."

We had just reached the front of the theater, which was no longer as dark and eerie as it had been. Close up, it was obvious to us that there was no screen at all. We climbed a few steep stairs to a dark stage, piled with various objects: old and new, small and large. Even the old things looked serviceable, if dusty, like the two-by-fours and roofing shingles scattered near the front.

"Will ya look at this stuff?" Tuck rummaged through the items, finding nuts and bolts, unrolling fabric and yarn, examining old boat equipment, and holding up a laptop that looked brand-new. "Look, Zia! I don't think this has ever been used! What I couldn't do with all this stuff—" He turned and looked at the back of the stage, which now appeared to extend farther back than it had on first inspection. "Zia, follow me! Look at all this *stuff*!" His excited voice became muffled as he walked further and further back. "Thank you thank you thank you for showing me this stage, woman!"

"I hear you, Tuck. I'm right here. Give me a sec and I'll join you." I stepped into the center of a huge coil of thick rope, intending to follow him, but at that precise moment, a door to the left of the stage opened; bright light poured into the dim space. I could see the outline of a figure, but couldn't make out the face.

"Hey, Zia." The figure was speaking to her, and she stopped, poised, one foot in the air. "We need you in here for a minute."

Surprised, not really sure who was asking me to come, but assuming it was part of my job, I said, "I'll be right there!"

The figure nodded, and walked back through the doorway, and I stepped out of the coiled rope. I couldn't see Tuck, so I called to him. "Hey, Tuck! I've got to run next door; I'm needed. Back in a few."

†

"Zia, you won't believe how cool this place is. It goes way, way back, this stage." Tuck's voice echoed in the quiet, dark theater.

"Zia?"

No light. No doors. No Zia. Tuck found himself alone again. He didn't cry. Instead, a wistful smile played on his lips as he looked toward the space where he had last seen her.

"Game on, Zia; *game on.*"

3

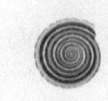

Tower

"I can't explain myself, I'm afraid, sir," said Alice,
"because I'm not myself, you see."
"I don't see," said the Caterpillar.
Lewis Carroll, *Alice's Adventures in Wonderland*

Curiouser and curiouser. People keep disappearing, just when things seem to be getting almost normal. Where the fuck did Zia go? I don't see any doors. But then, she didn't need a door to get in here, like I did. He stood, quite lost in thought, dangling in his right hand an orange electric drill he'd found among the plethora of items on the stage, his left hand rubbing the stubble on his chin and cheeks.

Tuck prided himself on being a rational man (in the world's meaning of a no-nonsense, strictly scientific, "show-me-or-blow-me" way), and in many aspects he was. He also possessed a penchant for profundity that few knew of, except Zia, and his eldest son. Often—especially when he had finished an arduous climb—he would sit on a remote ledge, thousands of feet above a valley, and just think. Sometimes he thought about how much he hated his life (except for the climbing and his kids), contrasting it to the change of perspective climbing gave him. As a wild teenager, he had worked summers as a trick water skier, and winters as a ski instructor (not beginners; he hated teaching beginners). He had had dreams of climbing Kilimanjaro, and being the first to ski from its heights; he had seen himself winning water skiing competitions all over the world, and having a beautiful girl in every port; he had wanted to own a ski resort in Utah—maybe even Alta!—and hang out with people like Robert Redford.

Instead, after high school he started working in his uncle's hardware store. It was meant to be temporary, but the months turned into years, and he worked his way up to head of sales. He met his wife when, undulating toward his counter and tossing her long black hair over one shoulder, she sidled up to him and asked for a large screw. He obliged her in both senses, first selling her a big brass one from stock, and then meeting her for drinks after he finished work, where he gave her the other one, in his '57 Pontiac. She ended up pregnant and the shotguns were hauled out of the closet.

Three children in as many years, and Tuck was finished with the stud business, getting himself fixed when his wife was away visiting her parents in Michigan. As far as he knew, she never knew; she did know, however, and that's when she stopped loving him. When his uncle died, he left Tuck the store. At the reading of the will, his siblings and parents were jealous of Tuck's good fortune; Tuck himself felt a profound depression.

The roar of the drill in his hand startled Tuck so much that he nearly fell off the stage.

"Jesus! he yelled. What the fuck...?" His innate sense of balance kept him from tumbling off the eight-foot-high stage into the tiny orchestra pit below. *Must've accidentally hit the trigger.* He depressed the trigger, twice. No whining sound, nothing at all. *Hmm. Must've been a little juice in the battery, and that was the last of it. Not good to keep batteries in it if you're not using it.* Mentally Tuck tsk-tsked the previous owner. With experienced fingers, he popped open the battery compartment. Both his eyebrows raised in surprise. *No batteries.* He stood there, holding the drill in both hands in front of him, looking at the empty compartment. Still holding the drill in the same way, he turned slowly on his right heel and surveyed the items on the stage. He slowly looked over his left shoulder to the place he'd last seen Zia. Turning his head back to the right, he looked carefully, deliberately, at what was in front of him. *A man like me could do a lot with these things. I might be able to build something to get me out of this place.*

Excitedly, he went over to the stack of two-by-fours. *Perfect. Seasoned wood, treated right. How many are there.* He calculated quickly. *Looks like at least twenty-four.* He started to the right, then stopped himself. *I'm sure I saw more of these way back on the stage, but these are enough to start with. Don't see a saw though.*

"Anybody see a saw? He laughed at his own wit. "Oh ye of such tiny wit and small," he misquoted gleefully.

"Isn't that supposed to be, 'He that has an' a little tiny wit'?" said another voice, a woman's.

Tuck dropped his drill in surprise, spinning around to discover the source of the voice. A woman with greasy blonde hair and a bewildered look stood eyeing him curiously. *Gerry's wife?*

"You scared the shit out of me! What are you doing here, uh…uh…" *Shit. What was her name?*

"Rosalie. My name's Rosalie. I'm Gerry's wife; you know Gerry?" She went right on, assuming he knew. "That line you messed up was from my kid's play. He musta said that line a million times. He was a Fool, I think." She stood there, holding a chainsaw.

"Is that the saw I sold you a couple years ago, the one you bought for Gerry's birthday?" Tuck couldn't believe his eyes.

"No…I mean, yeah, I bought it from you, but it was for Father's Day, not his birthday. I guess I did get it from you, Tuck, who else in town sells 'em? You have the only place in town I could get somethin' like this for my Gerry." She looked at the saw with genuine affection, as if it were an extension of her husband somehow.

"You were going to tell me how you got here," Tuck prompted.

"Was I? Sorry, I'm a little discombobulated here, Tuck. One minute I was making burgers for Gerry to put on the grill, and the next minute I'm here—"

She looked around uncertainly. "I'm in the old Rivoli?" Her down-to-earth, plodder's face showed utter incomprehension. "What are we doing in the old Rivoli, Tuck? I thought it was gonna be tore down this week." She looked at him for an explanation, holding the saw in both hands as if she might just cut him in two with it if he didn't give her a good answer.

Tuck thought quickly. *She's never gonna understand. Better just tell a little white lie here.*

"I'm here to do the work, the ah…restoration work. You know." He nodded hopefully. "I needed that saw, so I…" *Jesus, I can't just tell her that what I ask for appears, can I?* "I, ah, told Gerry last week if he had a chance to send down that saw, well, that'd be great. He must've told you to bring it here, right?" Tuck flashed the fake smile. It worked.

"Yeah, Tuck, that must be it. I musta forgot he sent me." She nodded and smiled uncertainly, but figuring it must be true if Tuck said it. He was real enough, and so was this heavy saw in her hands. In her small world, she could envision nothing strange or unworldly ever occurring.

"Can I have the saw now?" Tuck held out his hands, wary of approaching her in case she changed her mind and decided to attack him, fake smile or no fake smile.

"Uh, sure, Tuck." She stretched out her arms and he came, on tiptoe, to rescue the saw. He didn't want that thing starting up on its own, like the drill had, and she was standing there looking up, down, all around, at the darkened theater, her lank blond hair lagging behind the rest of her head.

"Pretty dark in here, Tuck. Why's it so dark in here?" Her voice strained through her elongated neck. She peered straight up, something Tuck hadn't thought of doing yet. He looked up, too.

"Is that a hole in the roof there, Tuck? I think it might be sunshine I see up there. Whaddya think, Tuck? Ya might wanna fix that first, it's sposeta rain tonight."

"You might be right there, Rosalie. Thank you for spotting that." *She is right! That's sunshine up there. Fuckin' A!* "How far up do you reckon that is? Thirty, forty foot?"

Silence.

Tuck's neck jerked stageward. *Damn! I forgot to ask her what time it was. And what day.* Tuck sighed. One of these times, he'd remember to ask. *Well, at least I've got the saw. And a way out.* He chuckled. The look on her face had been priceless. Whistling, he went to the pile of two-by-fours and picked the sturdiest-looking one.

†

Tuck wiped the sweat from his brow with a piece of bright fabric. He glowed with pride at his creation, a tower almost fifty feet high (forty-eight, to be exact). He had constructed the base out of four old fishing boats, secured to a platform he had made out of some of the myriad two-by-fours on the stage. He had patiently ripped out most of the theater's center seats, saving the wrought-iron chair legs' bolts for use on the tower's girders, again using more two-by-fours, but welded with aluminum from the store of pots and pans he'd discovered next to an old WC.

It was a happy day, the one when he'd found the disused toilet. He'd fixed it up for his own use, along with a tiny kitchenette with a pantry full of canned goods. Once, when he was in the kitchenette, a Culligan man had appeared, asking where he wanted him to put the twenty, five-gallon jugs of water he had with him. *Anywhere you'd like, man; anywhere you'd like. Thanks.* And the Culligan man disappeared, too, before Tuck had had a chance to ask any questions.

Tuck had decided to build a tower with what he'd found on stage. To secure it as he worked on it, he came up with a guy wire system, attaching the wire to pitons he placed in the wall. He'd discovered that the gaudy crimson-flocked wallpaper actually covered cement walls that could, with considerable effort, be drilled to hold the pitons he'd found in abundance under an old parachute. He'd found great coils of cable, as well as rope; he used the cable to tie the tower pieces together, and the rope to climb up with, rappelling down after each day's work.

The funny thing was, the roof was deceptively far away. Tuck would think he was about ten feet from it, but the next time he climbed up, it would look more like twenty. The roof was a sort of rotunda; from Tuck's perspective you could see the remains of beautiful artwork. *Maybe it's* trump-de-lie. *I bet I'm pronouncing that wrong. Zia would tell me.* He half-laughed. *Maybe Rosalie could tell me!* It was painted to look like a huge spiraly shell, with faded figures of Greek or Roman gods and goddesses painted on it. If Tuck looked from another angle, though, it reminded him of one of Zia's tarot cards. He'd had to think which one it was, then it came to him. *The Wheel of Fortune. That was it. ROTA. Or was it TORA? Maybe that was the point; it could go either way.* He wished he could remember more of what she'd told him, those nights they'd spent in front of the fire; he'd drink and she would do a Tarot reading. But back then, his mind was more on how to get her incredibly responsive body into the sack than on hokey Tarot claptrap. *Might've come in handy now, though. Zia would know what those paintings on the ceiling meant.*

Standing at the base of the tower, though, the rotunda was pretty blurry. *You only see how pretty it is when you're close up. Too hard to tell from a distance.* He clapped his hands once and then rubbed them together.

"Okay, Tuck m'boy, time to climb El Cap!" He'd nicknamed the tower after his favorite mountain. He'd also taken to talking out loud to himself, once he'd realized that if he needed anything, it would show up more quickly if he spoke up instead of just thinking it. Climbing the tower each day, using the pulley he'd made to haul up needed materials, he even sang (in his dreadful voice) all the songs he could remember. He talked to his children as if they were there, dispensing sage advice and patiently answering their questions. *I've sorta built a different life, from the ground up*, he would say to them, in his thoughts.

One day, when he had climbed halfway up the tower, he looked up at the receding rotunda. *In one way, I don't even care if I reach the top.* He hung there, suspended, gently swinging from the strong rope. Like he used to do mid-climb, he fished out the tobacco-weed mixture and rolled himself a joint. He allowed himself to close his eyes and, after taking a nice long toke, imagine he was not twenty-four, but twenty-four hundred feet from the ground. He imagined the sun gently warming the top of his helmet, while his breath formed little vapor clouds from the cold, and his chalk-covered, stiff fingers held his smoke. He imagined he looked out at Lake Superior from his eagle's height, soaking in the stupendous beauty of the North Shore. His climbing buddy tugged on his rope.

"Come down here, Tuck. You're needed."

That doesn't sound like Greg. The rope moved in his hands. *Holy shit, that's Zia!* "Am I seeing things, or is that you, Zia?" He wasn't sure of anything, except that she was more beautiful than those faded goddesses on the rotunda above him.

Her smile rose from within, lit by some fire he could not see. Her multicolored skirt swirled around her. As he rappelled toward her, savoring her beauty, he noticed how her purple blouse made her eyes look like emeralds. He descended slowly, not wanting to lose the magic of this moment—in case it was only a dream.

She waited with her left hand stretched toward him. When he landed, he started undoing the tool belt, but she shook her head.

"You'll need everything you've got with you," she said. Joyful, she took my hand and led me through a door that stood open, to the left of the stage.

4

Mountain

How long a time lies in one little word!
Four lagging winters and four wanton springs
End in a word; such is the breath of kings.
Shakespeare, *Richard II*

Tuck found himself with a rope in his hands, on a sheer-granite, steep ascent, a piton glinting about six feet away, but slightly to the right, at an awkward angle. Clouds roiled and bubbled greyly a thousand feet above him, clouds that held snow—not rain. Judging by the way he was breathing, he had to be higher than twelve thousand feet. He felt the way he had on Macchu Pichu, gasping for breath for three days before his body's red corpuscles increased to the point that his lungs could accommodate the thin air. *What am I doing on a climb like this? This is at least a 5.12, maybe more. And those clouds are trouble. I don't like the look of them at all. It looks like I'm lead climber, too. What was I thinking when I took this gig?*

A violent tug on the rope caused him to look down. *Shit. I'm leading at least one…*another helmeted head came into view…*make that two…*then another…*you must be kidding. Three more people?* He hefted a small section of rope cautiously. *At least the rope's good. Excellent quality. Strong and sinuous. Tibetan?*

He didn't have time to think about the rope any more. From above he heard the sound that mountaineers fear nearly as much as the roar of an avalanche: rocks. Only a trained ear could detect, sliding in and out of the wind's howl, that slight *ch-ch-ch-ch-chhhh* sound that signaled stones were heading down the mountain. Because the sound was increasing rapidly, Tuck could tell the stones would be on top of them shortly.

He pulled three times, slowly but firmly, on the rope, the signal he hoped they understood meant that a rock slide was on its way. Then he yelled, keeping the left side of his head flush with the granite, "Rock slide! Keep your head in close!" *What the fuck?! What language am I speaking? Did I say that?* He tried again. "Don't climb any more! Rocks!" *What language is this?* A quick glance down to the climber still struggling upward alerted Tuck that his message either had not been heard—or had been heard but not understood. The climber continued his ascent.

There was no more time for warnings anyway. The shower of rocks was, literally, upon them. *Breathe deep, Tuck m'boy. Become part of the mountain. Melt right in. The rocks won't even see you. Melt in.* Still and calm, Tuck waited. He felt the rush of air as a large one, probably half his weight, skidded an inch or so from his right arm. He felt no further tugs on the rope. *I hope those guys flattened themselves against the mountain. Probably did; I would've felt something otherwise.*

As quickly as it had started, it was over. There was one further *ping* on his helmet from a tiny stone, and that was it. "All clear!" he yelled, again, in a language he could not understand. Glancing down, he could see thumbs-up signs from the two climbers in view. He gave a tug on the rope, and began the ascent again.

First we need to get to that hold. Looks like there's a ledge above it. He tried to gauge the distance, and how he would get the others up there. *If this route already has fixed ropes, somebody had to put them in. I hope to god it was me. Then I'd know it was done right.*

It took an hour for the climbers to reach the ledge, which fortunately was more sizeable than Tuck had first thought. The first man to reach the ledge after him gestured his inability to understand a word Tuck spoke, shaking his head, then pointing his heavily gloved hand downwards, and repeating the word "Charles." *All right already, I get it! The guy's name is Charles and you don't understand a word I'm saying.* Tuck marveled, though, at his own ability to understand the American sharing the ledge, an American wearing some very old-fashioned climbing gear. When the next man arrived, dressed in the same outdated clothes, the first pointed to him excitedly, saying, "Charles! Charles!" *I hope this guy is an interpreter.* To Tuck's relief, Charles spoke in the new language, too.

"Art doesn't understand you, Sherpa. Talk to me only, remember? I'll do the translating for you." Then he turned to Art with a laugh muffled by his balaclava, and scarf, shaking his head, pointing at Tuck, and saying, "We've been on this expedition, what, eight days? He still doesn't have it through his thick head that you don't understand Pakistani. These people may be great climbers, but they're so stupid."

Tuck, stung by Charles' remarks, nonetheless appreciated the clue to where they were. If he was Pakistani, that could mean he was leading a team up K2. *I wish I could see better. I'd know where we were.* The other two climbers finally made it to the safety of the ledge, and not a moment too soon. A heavy mist was gathering thickly around them, cutting visibility to nearly zero. Insult or no insult, Tuck wanted to leave the mountain alive and in one piece, so he addressed Charles.

Putting aside his dislike, he said, "It would be a good idea to listen to what I have to say. I may be the only one who can get you off this mountain alive. We can climb no further today, and from the looks of the weather, we will need to abandon the climb altogether. We can stay on this ledge until morning. Let's make camp." He fumbled with the leather bag strapped to his belt in an attempt to open it and get the tent out. He was appalled to see, not the lightweight Patagonian kit he favored, but crude gear made of another fabric. *Jesus, is this parachute silk?* He couldn't take off his gloves to find out, but it sure looked like a parachute. *And wool socks? They'll never dry out up here! And where's the Sterno?* He was distracted from his frantic search of the kit bag with something far more chilling. He heard Charles "interpret" his advice for the others.

"... so basically, we're going to wait it out here for a while and see if it clears up. If it does, we're going to push on up the mountain," said Charles, gesturing as he spoke. "If not, there's another ledge a little further up and we can stay there for the night, right Sherpa?" Tuck couldn't see Charles' mouth, but he could see, even in the heavy mist, how Charles' stony eyes had narrowed to slits.

"That's not what I said, and you know it," said Tuck, his voice deep and threatening. "Disregard my advice, and we could all die." He gestured to the other men. "Go on; tell them the truth. Do you want to be responsible for their deaths? These guys don't know how to climb well enough to make it to the top, and you know it." He gestured to the traverse they'd just made. "Did you see how long it took them to make that climb?"

The other climbers listened intently, understanding the tone, if not the words, of Tuck's message. When Tuck finished, they looked, wide-eyed and questioning, at Charles. Charles looked at Tuck for a long moment, then at his fellow mountaineers. "Sherpa says we can do it, guys. We might sit here for a while, but then it's onward and upward. Go USA!" They gave a little cheer, clapping their gloved hands together. To Tuck, Charles said, "Don't you *ever* undermine my authority again, you Pakistani git. We paid a lot of money for this expedition—for *you*—and we're going to the top. I tried to do it last year and failed, but I'm not failing this time." Tuck's heart—and hopes—sank. He was on a mountain with a mad man.

†

They spent the night huddled under parachute silk as the wind howled around them and snow fell. Tuck found out that some of their supplies, including most of their water, had been lost during the rock slide; the bag holding them had split in two from the impact. *Somehow I've got to convince them to abandon this climb. It'll be tough enough to head back as it is, and I don't even know how I got up here.* Tuck had never been the praying type, but he prayed now. He knew he could not go back on his own, abandoning them to certain death, yet he also knew the team was not capable of climbing further up the mountain. He spent a fitful night on the ledge, cold and hungry. Apparently Pakistanis were expected to survive on less food—or no food, as on this occasion—than Americans.

A weak light crept under Tuck's eyelids, awakening him. He pulled up a corner of the makeshift tent, surveying the surrounding scene. Sunlight struggled to pierce the dense clouds high above; it looked like it might win. The snow had stopped at some point during the night, and only a fine powder, maybe an inch thick, covered the flat surfaces. Luckily, the fixed rope was still visible, and the slope appeared dry. *If they see this weather, they're going to want to climb up. We need to take advantage of this weather and move* down, *though. Well, here goes.*

Tuck shook each of the men in turn. "Tell 'em it's time to go, Charles. Time to go *down* the mountain, back to safety. I don't know how long this weather will hold." He hoped he had said this with enough authority to make Charles see sense.

"Time to go, guys." Charles shook each of them. "C'mon! Rise and shine!" Charles shook the fellow called Art more vigorously. "Art! C'mon buddy. Wakey-wakey." Art didn't respond, slumping over to one side. "Jesus," Charles said, his voice shaking. "Jesus. C'mon Art, c'mon old buddy." No response.

Tuck managed to remove his thick glove, trying to get to Art's neck to feel for a pulse. Charles, seeing what Tuck was trying to do, helped as best he could, pawing away at the thick wool scarves and trying to unzip Art's parka. The cold seeped into Tuck's fingers so rapidly, he could barely feel them. There was no warmth under the parka, or the scarves: it took only a few seconds to determine that Art was dead. Quickly, he put on his own glove again, before frostbite could set in.

"He's dead," Tuck confirmed. "We cannot take him down the mountain. Surely you saw on our way up the skeletons of those who have tried this ascent and failed?" Charles, bowing his head slightly, nodded. "The best thing we can do," Tuck continued, is take as many of Art's supplies with us as possible, especially his food." Not to sound too cold-hearted, but wanting to move off the mountain as soon as possible, Tuck added, "Charles, maybe you would say a prayer for Art, and let the mountain have him."

Charles nodded again, contrite at last. The climber named Peter, probably the least experienced of them, looked from Charles to Tuck, and back at Charles, a terrified expression in his eyes. "Peter, Art is dead. We're going to go back down the mountain now, after I say a little prayer for Art." He took a deep breath, blowing it out slowly through his ski mask. "We're going to take Art's food and climbing gear with us." He saw the stricken look in Peter's eyes. "Peter, did he have a picture of his wife with him, or anything like that?" Peter nodded dumbly, gesturing toward Art's upper jacket pocket.

Charles said a few words, commending Art to K2. *I was right. It's K2. Good ol' Savage Mountain.* Tuck thought for a moment, pursing his chapped lips under the heavy scarf. *I think we're on the Albruzzi Spur. From the looks of our gear, this must be the early 1950s, so it's before the Northeast Ridge route was found. I think I can get us down from here.* With more confidence than he felt, he motioned to the others to pack as much gear as they could, and then they began the fearful descent to base camp.

They were only about eight hundred feet from safety when it happened. Charles was in the lead, Peter second, and Tuck last, pulling back their rope and removing pitons. Charles slipped, causing him to drop twenty feet; at the same time, Tuck had removed a piton, leaving his rope end momentarily unsecured. The violence of Charles' fall caused Tuck to drop more than sixty feet, slamming into granite outcroppings. Both men were now dangling from either end of the rope to which Peter was secured by a single piton.

Tuck was dazed and concussed from his fall. He couldn't hear Peter shouting directions to Charles, who tried to tell Tuck. Using superhuman strength, Peter somehow raised Charles to a small ledge where he could balance until both men could lower Tuck to safety.

†

When they reached him later, as he lay on the wide rock's ledge, Tuck was still clinging to the end of the rope, stroking it and kissing it. He was saying something, over and over, that Charles was at a loss to interpret, for the word did not mean "rope."

"Zia...Zia...Zia."

5

Rescue

Faith consists in believing when it is beyond the power of reason to believe.
It is not enough that a thing be possible for it to be believed.
Voltaire, *Questions sur l'Encyclopédie*

Tuck tried to move. He felt taller, sinuous, but he ached along his entire length. He seemed to be lying against rough fabric, on something or someone far larger—or at least wider—than himself, and through which he could feel distinctly, depending on which part of him was touching: a solid, rough surface, like wood; warmth; wetness; more wood; warmth again; more wood; more warmth; more wood (smaller, thinner now); straw; earth. *Maybe I'm not human, even though I hurt like one.*

He could hear a muffled drum, beating the same rhythm, quickly, repeatedly. *Ta-t-tum, ta-t-tum, ta-t-tum, ta-t-tum.* It soothed him, relieving somewhat his aches and pains. He wasn't able to bring his arms down, or his feet up (*maybe I don't have any*); still, it was not wholly unpleasant. He felt long, and strong—in the best shape of his life, in fact. *There must be no buttered popcorn around. Won't have to worry about my weight.* He had to admit, he didn't feel hungry anyway.

Instead of bringing his arms down, he thought he'd try rolling. *Aha! I can do that at least.* He opened his eyes—to the strangest sight he'd ever seen. *What the fuck?* It was like peering through one elongated peephole, about a quarter-inch thick. From what he was seeing, his eye length matched the peephole's. And from this peephole, he saw, looking from right to left: sky (blue); rope (*thick—good stuff*); hair (*ooh, red—very nice*); skin (*must be the neck*); more skin, but a little damp; some soft lace followed by brown, suede-ish fabric (*am I going where I hope I'm going?*); what looked like a small mountain, soft (*nice tit—that drum sound's louder here, must be the heart*); people (*hmm, dressed funny, standing sideways*); wood (*what size's this? bigger'n a two-by-four, not sawed very well*); more rope (*I feel a little dizzy*); a flash of green grass (*needs mowing*); rough cotton covering a large, firm mound (*oh, nice ass*); over more cotton (*I'd recognize that smell anywhere!*); more sky; more grass (*that's a lot closer than before*); sticks; straw; two human feet in weird leather slippers; that big chunk of wood again; and (*ow! watch what you're doing, bucko! ow-w-w-w*) fingers-palm-fingers-wood-fingers-sky-wood-grass-straw-fingers in quick succession. *I'm not human any more. That's a given. The question is, What am I?*

He found he could isolate his vision by concentrating on one section of his curled self at a time. *Much as I'd love to stay with those tits, I'm going to have to concentrate elsewhere.* He tried speaking out loud, but nothing came out except a small *ree-er* sound, inaudible, apparently, even to the woman whose body he seemed attached to in some way. The grass area made him dizzy, so he shifted his awareness to near the red hair. The people were at a slant, but he could hear pretty well. They were gathered for something or other. He could glimpse the blue sky, and he could smell the woman's hair, comforting and familiar. He thought he'd stay there; it wasn't as distracting as some of her other smells and features.

There were a lot of people, and judging from the way their sounds ebbed and flowed, they were in a circle. Ignoring the tickle at the straw end, Tuck saw Shoes move briefly into his range of vision, this time catching a glimpse of Shoes's stout body, too. There was much shushing, and Tuck heard a voice, a voice whose words let him know one thing for sure: someone was in trouble. He sure hoped it wasn't the woman whose body he was next to.

"Hear ye, hear ye. All quiet for the Judge."

That shut 'em up.

A man's form flitted briefly across Tuck's vision.

"It is my grave duty," the voice continued, "as the Judge appointed by His Royal Highness King James (may God bless him forever) for Essex County and thereby for the village of Hanby-on-Trent, to oversee the punishment to be meted out to the prisoner on this Day of Our Lord, the Eighth of September, in the Year of Our Lord, 1601.

Talk about being a part of history. I'm not sure I want this part. Tuck, putting together the things he had learned about himself in the last ten minutes, couldn't help but continue listening. *I may as well know what's going to happen to me. I hate surprises.* He tried some gallows humor—*how did I get roped into this?*—but it didn't help. Not at all.

"Are you the woman called Zia, of the family Dawson, of the County of Essex, Village of Hanby-on-Trent, who has been tried and found guilty by the Grand Inquisitor of that most heinous crime, witchcraft?"

Stunned, Tuck felt her answer resonate in every sinew of himself:

"*Yes*, I am that Zia Dawson, but I am not a witch. I am a wise woman and healer."

The man shouted at her. "SILENCE! You are to state 'yes' or "no" only. The time for defending yourself has passed." The man paused before saying words at which Tuck trembled, along with Zia:

"You shall now be burned at the stake in punishment for your crimes. Will the Fire Starter please move to the stake and begin the burning."

The crowd cheered, but Tuck could still hear Zia's heart above the din. He could feel her as he stretched around her form, from her beautiful hair, to her neck where the tears ran freely onto him now, around her breasts, her hips, her thighs. He felt the ponderous steps of the Fire Starter as the man advanced over the uneven grass toward them.

Zia! Zia! Zia! He willed her to feel him against her. "Tuck?" she whispered, unbelievingly. "Tuck? Are you here? Where are you? I feel you." The red hair swished one way, then the other, over him. Tuck could see Shoes. He smelled, rather than saw, the burning faggot as it touched first twig, then straw. He could feel warmth at the grass end of himself; not painful, exactly, just very warm. *I will save you, Zia.*

Tuck concentrated with his every fiber. He envisioned each sinew unraveling, unknotting. *Hot. Jesus, but it's hot. Must keep going. C'mon Tuck. C'mon boy. You can do it.* He collapsed in a heap, now burning and melting. The pain was so intense, Tuck could not hear the cries of the crowd; he could not hear the Judge, dumbfounded, exonerating Zia, declaring her to be a saint, not a witch. God had undone the rope that bound her, the Judge said; she walked away from the fire unscathed because God willed it so. If God did not want her dead, reasoned the Judge, far be it from him to punish her.

Then Tuck felt a hand—*her* hand—gently close itself around his sky-end and pull what was left of him from the flames. On her knees, in the green grass, she rocked him, holding him with both hands tightly between her heaving breasts, scooping his still-smoldering grass-end into her soft lap while her tears, her copious tears, washed him.

6

Teosinte

I have called this principle, by which each slight variation,
if useful, is preserved, by the term of Natural Selection.
Charles Darwin, *The Origin of the Species*

Tuck looked up at the small, gray clouds hovering on the mountain tops surrounding him. *It just might rain tomorrow, if those clouds are anything to go by. A little rain could go a long way. This crop could use it.* He examined the plant he held in his hands, a sort of mini-corn on the cob, bearing eight rows of kernels. He had just plucked it from the tended field he stood in under the hot sun. He ran his large thumb over the tightly packed, hard-as-rock buds. He surveyed the scene around him again. To his left, in the limited shade afforded by the towering mountain behind it, stood a rude dwelling; a hut, really. It was composed of a mixture of earth that had been roughly shaped into a type of brick, and stones that must have come from the mountain. He walked over to it now, walking slowly, thoughtfully, as he tried to get a sense of where he was.

There was no sidewalk of any description; only a well-worn path from the door of the hut to the field. A bell tinkled loudly, just off to his right, and Tuck, startled, turned toward the sound. A white, horned goat came from behind the hut, munching on a tuft of grass he must have gone a long way to find. It came up to him, first nuzzling for affection, which Tuck instinctively gave him, rubbing the narrow space between the goat's eyes, down to its quivering nose. Tuck, lost in thought, did not realize the goat had stopped nuzzling and was instead nibbling on his clothing. When he felt the tug of cloth entering maw, he quickly looked down, pushing the goat away hurriedly.

"Stop that, Billy!" he said, and then nearly choked. *I'm speaking another language again!* Tuck tested his voice again: "My name is Tuck. Two plus two is four. I don't understand what's happening." He said each word loudly and slowly, trying to figure out what language he might be speaking, but to no avail. *Sounds a little like Spanish, but it's too harsh, too guttural. Damn. Well, I guess it doesn't matter—doesn't look like anyone's here to talk to anyway.*

From where he stood, Tuck could see no signs of any human being there but himself. His hut, he noticed, had a small plume of smoke rising from a tiny chimney near the back. Nowhere else could he spot a matching plume, nor did it look like there were any wheel tracks or paths, other than the one from his front door to the small patch of land growing the strange grain. *Or whatever it is.* Still, he did not feel lonely. Instead, he felt an inner peace and calm, almost a happiness, something he didn't remember ever experiencing. Surrounded by the majestic, craggy peaks and rich foreign earth, he felt at home.

After standing, silent, for a time, Tuck made for the hut. *Time to see what's inside.* Before he went through the doorway (if it could be called that; there was no door, just animal pelts he had to part to enter), he ran his hand over the hut's exterior, closing his eyes and letting his fingers rest on each little tuft of dried grass or lump of dried mud he touched. *I built this.* He suddenly remembered: he could see himself, sweating under a steamy sun, mixing water and sand and clay and grass—dried first on the ground outside his hut. He saw himself forming the bricks and laying them out in the sun to dry. He was naked to the waist, with only a loincloth to cover him. He opened his eyes, smiling. *This is home.*

He sensed what would lie behind the animal-pelt door before he saw it. He closed his eyes again, standing just inside the entry, and played the little game he did when he climbed. He would sense where things were by listening to how sound—like the wind, the rain, a voice—would bounce off the surfaces near him. On several occasions in his life, whether as a rescue skier or lead climber, he had used this technique to find a safe route out of wherever he found himself. The hut, he sensed, posed no danger, and he would be able to do this just for fun.

"Teosinte!"

Tuck's eyes flew open and he staggered back through the doorway a few steps, tripping on the rough lintel and landing on his behind before he could take another breath. The woman whose voice had startled him appeared in the doorway, laughing gently, the sound like a rivulet over small rocks in a deep forest. She used her hands to support herself as she rocked gently forward and back at the threshold, laughing softly.

Tuck could only stare: she was perfection itself. His eyes traveled from her long, thick, black hair—hair that fell past her rounded, full breasts almost to her waist—to her hips which undulated gently, and the creamy chocolate thighs flashing, first the left one, then the right, from beneath a sort of skirt made of soft pelts not unlike those that made up the door to his home. Her feet were bare, with dainty toes and trimmed nails. Some of the toes had silver rings, he noticed. *I made those for her.* His eyes traveled back up her exquisite body, this time noticing that she had other jewelry—necklaces, bracelets, rings—adorning her as well.

"Zia! Don't laugh!" He found himself laughing with her, though. *I must have called her the right name.* He didn't understand any other of the words she spoke, but when her dark eyes began to smolder and her laughter stopped, he knew exactly what she was saying. His body responded instantly and she came to him, full of desire. His loincloth had fallen to one side, and she lowered herself on him. As she moaned with delight, his hands reached for her full breasts, massaging them reverently. There, in the sun and the thin mountain air, with the goat watching and nibbling nearby, Tuck knew why he was happy here on this mountain. Tears of joy misted his eyes as he and Zia looked at each other.

After their love-making, they stood together, his right arm around her small waist, and her left arm around his slim one. Zia was pointing toward the field, gesturing first toward the sky, then downward, down the mountain toward the north. *It would be nice to know what she was saying. God, her hair smells like wood smoke and junipers and…*

Her arm had left his waist and her hand was now pulling him toward the field. She had a light step and fairly danced toward the patch of ground, taking him with her. He just wanted to watch her swively hips—so enticing— but she wouldn't let him. Chattering animatedly, she snatched up some of the strange grass, running her fingers over the tiny kernels, gesturing with her hands. He caught some of her enthusiasm, realizing she was excited about their crop. *She keeps pointing down the mountain. Maybe there's a village there, or someone she wants to show this to.*

Still holding the grain in her dainty left hand, she pulled him back up toward the hut with her right, and began running. Breathless, she went to the small hearth on the right side of their home, showing him the food she had made. *If she wants me to eat it, why doesn't she just give it to me? I'm starving.* She was pointing to the grain, then to the big stones near the fire, then at the makeshift grill poised over the fire, then to the flattish bread placed next to it. She broke off a piece of the bread and fed it to him. *Not bad. I get it; she must have taken the grain, pounded the hell out of it into a powder, then mixed it with water and made this bread.* He looked at her with pride.

"You're amazing, Zia!" This time he didn't stop to hear the sound of his own voice, he just kept talking, the words tumbling out, and Zia appearing to understand everything, even if he didn't. "You've discovered how to turn this grass or grain or whatever it is into an edible food! How did you know it wouldn't kill you?" He looked at her with love, and he felt desire rise in him again. Hers must have too, as she dropped the grain and the bread, enveloping him in her warm brown arms and smothering his face with kisses. They didn't make it to the pelt-covered mat that served as their bed; they just made love on the swept dirt floor of the hut. This time there was no audience, for the goat stayed outside.

†

That night Tuck dreamed. Lying there next to Zia, he had fallen asleep feeling the warmth of her back against that of his chest and abdomen, with his hand draped casually over her shoulder.

In his dream, he was walking—walking through a green meadow, filled with flowers and plants not unlike the new grain in his garden. The meadow's ground rose steadily, and Tuck kept walking, swinging his arms in time with his happy steps. There was a rise ahead of him, but so far the way was not difficult; he climbed it easily and stood on the moss and grass-covered rise, looking out over the green meadows and fields through which he had walked so easily, so happily. Behind him and to the right, a snow-covered mountain towered above the valley and the rise upon which Tuck stood. A huge forest began near the bottom of the rise on which he stood, stretching toward and up the mountain until the air became too thin for trees, and only the scrubby junipers could survive.

Between the forest and where the rise began flowed a sparkling river. He followed with his eyes the path the river had taken to get this far; he could see it glinting far, far up the mountain. The melted snow tumbled down the mountain, picking up speed and strength as it came, and bringing with it a cool breeze and a fresh, clean smell.

As he stood on the rise, gazing out at the beauty around him, clouds gathered at the mountain's summit, blocking out the sun as it headed toward the midpoint of the sky. The ground shook beneath him, violently, throwing him to his knees. Behind him, he saw a stone altar appear as if by magic from beneath the carpet of grass and flowers covering the rise. As if a giant finger were drawing in the sand, a trough appeared around the base of the altar. A giant, unseen finger drew a new course for the nearby stream, bringing it rushing past where Tuck sat, dazed, on the ground. He heard drums beating in the distance, from the direction he had traveled. It looked like an army—solemn, dark-skinned men wearing loincloths, and with their faces painted in frightening colors, advanced toward the rise where Tuck knelt.

In front of this army were a group of men bearing a richly decorated palanquin. As they marched closer, he saw it was adorned with fine silks and jewels, in colors fiery and bright—reds, golds, oranges. He knew, in his dream, that whoever was in the palanquin was to be sacrificed, and they were coming to the altar—the altar by which he sat—to complete their rites.

Suddenly, the horde was there, on the rise, at least, as many as could fit there at one time. The columns of men stretched into the distance for as far as Tuck could see. Everywhere they had walked, the foliage both under their feet and within twenty feet of their columns was charred, burned, dead. A trail of destruction led to the spot where Tuck sat watching, mesmerized. It seemed they did not know he was there, for no one looked his way or acknowledged his presence. The palanquin was brought to the edge of the altar, just in front of the trough which encircled it. Two handsome men opened the white silky curtains that had disguised the palanquin's occupant.

At first, no one came out. It was only after the man Tuck assumed was the chief barked an order in a tongue he did not understand that the young men helped the stunning, beautiful woman out of the palanquin.

In the dream, Tuck gasped, for it was Zia—his Zia. Her long, thick, black hair was decorated with heather and corn blossoms; she was naked but for a leather pouch dangling from a belt she wore low, around her perfect hips. She did not cry; she was strong and brave; she knew there was no sense in crying. She walked to the altar herself, and was helped onto it by the two young men. She laid down, her feet toward the front of the round altar, facing the army.

Then Tuck heard another sound, one that caused him to shift his gaze from Zia. Someone else was coming out of the palanquin. It was a child, a small boy, maybe four or five years old. In the dream, the boy looked like him—Tuck. The child was crying silently and saying, "Mama! Mama!" The child was taken over to the far side of the altar, away from Tuck, and held back by the two other young men.

The chief walked up to the altar, carrying a huge machete. He raised it high over his head, standing over Zia's naked body. The sun broke through the clouds, making the scene more garish with its brightness. The knife swooped down, slicing Zia in half. The chief reached in, grabbed the still beating heart, and held it up to the sun, now directly above the grisly scene.

The little boy screamed, stretching his arm and holding out his hand, stretching and stretching toward his mother, to no avail—

†

"What is it, my love?" Tuck awoke to see Zia's anxious face beside his, her eyes wide with concern. Tuck realized, because his throat was raw, that he had been screaming too, and he had soaked their bedding with his sweat. His hand was still stretched taut in the air, and he, seeing that he had only been dreaming, lowered his hand, placing it instead on his wife's soft cheek.

"It was only a dream, Zia. Only a dream." For the rest of the night, she draped her left arm tightly around his chest, her right hand stroked his hair, and her lips kissed his forehead gently.

†

By watching Zia's gestures and listening intently, Tuck began to make sense of her language—their language. Zia did not seem surprised at his long silences and the frequent sage head-noddings he used whenever he didn't understand. *I must've been doing this a lot already.* He nodded as she showed him her latest bread making effort. *I think I'm starting to learn the language, though.* Tuck had never thought of himself as someone who could learn a new language, but it appeared he was doing all right. And as far as the language of love—well, there he needed no coaching. He and Zia made love whenever the mood struck them, which was often. *I wonder how long we've been together. It must be a pretty new thing if it's this good all the time.*

After several weeks of Zia patiently repeating the movements Tuck had seen her make on his first day, he understood that she wanted him to go down the mountain and bring the corn—for lack of a better word, that's what he called it—with him. Zia thought he should show it, and the bread she'd made from it, to the Chief of a village somewhere in the valley. It appeared that the trip might take a few days; Zia began packing bedding and supplies, and gesturing that he should help her do so. Two sturdy goat-hide bags, rather like saddlebags, were filled with provisions for the journey. She expertly rolled up a large, spare hide, which Tuck assumed would be his sleeping bag; she also packed a rope made of a fiber he didn't recognize, and a small, shovel-like instrument made of stone. In the bag she placed two large smooth rocks, which would serve to grind the corn, and a leather water pouch was filled from the small stream that ran just a quarter of a mile from their dwelling.

Tuck, by watching Zia since he'd arrived, had learned which berries and nuts were edible, and knew now where to find them; they must have comprised their diet before Zia discovered how to grind the corn. Tuck packed flints, but no tinder—there would be plenty of that in the undergrowth.

When Zia added the precious corn and samples of bread to one saddlebag, Tuck knew it was time to go. Dawn crept over the rim of the mountain as they embraced one last time before he left. Though both of them were filled with the desire to make love, they knew Tuck's journey could not be delayed. He needed all the daylight hours these long summer days could give him.

"Come back to me, Teosinte," she murmured in his ear, and giving him a quick soft kiss.

"Yes, Zia; yes." Tuck thought he said, "I love you" then, because it was something he had heard her say to him. But what he actually said in the strange tongue was, "I am with you always, like the sun."

He started down the mountain, Billy by his side, the saddlebags attached by a strong, woven ribbon over the goat's back. Little silver cymbals decorated the bags and jingled bravely in the cool, thin air. A lump rose in Tuck's throat; he turned to see Zia, gently waving both hands in farewell, her white teeth gleaming in her smile. He waved, too, his mind etching her beautiful body into his memory—only without the tears streaming down her lovely face.

†

There were few trees, and those were scrubby junipers, near Tuck's farm; as Tuck walked further down the steep mountain, however, the number and types of trees increased. A path of sorts had revealed itself just past his field, but it was obvious it hadn't been used much. Only the goats' grazing had kept it visible at all. He had discovered that he and Zia owned half a dozen goats, which roamed the remote area near their home, and provided the bulk of what he and Zia needed to live. He liked hearing their soft bells jingle in the early morning as he and Zia laid on their fur-pelt bed.

Now, as Tuck made his way down the mountain, the sun climbed higher in the summer sky. Numerous trees provided some measure of shade, but Tuck was still sweating profusely. The path abruptly turned left, and after a few steps he realized why he had to travel in daylight. There, spread before him in its majesty, rippled a valley, glittering green and blue in the hazy heat. He was on a narrow, stony path: in back of him was sheer rock jutting upwards; a few feet in front of him, the cliff sheared off into a series of valleys far below.

"Whoa, Billy, will you look at that?" Tuck whistled in admiration. Before them rose mountain after mountain, a 3–D tapestry of earth and sky, with no human in sight. On the closest slopes he could see some goats, however, signs that someone—maybe someone like him—was living out there.

"Let's stop here for a minute, Billy. You go get something to eat." Tuck took out one of the flints, scraped together some tinder, and then took what looked like a small cigar from the pouch tied to the belt at his waist. He had watched Zia gather green leaves from a plant he'd never seen, chop them and dry them in the sun, and then roll the mixture tightly in a large, fresh leaf.

She would then light it from the embers of the constant fire in their hearth. She would often become ecstatic—as well as more romantic, if that was possible—after smoking these leaves. After watching her do it a few times, he began to roll his own, and the two of them would sit in a wondrous stupor together. Tuck would often have visions, but there was nothing to write them down with—or on—so he just kept them in his head.

He sat now, his legs dangling from the cliff's edge, smoking and admiring the stupendous view. He took a sip of the cool, clear water from the goatskin canteen at his side, closing his eyes and feeling the liquid slide from the back of his tongue, and down his esophagus to his stomach, where it rested, cool and pure. He breathed the aromatic smoke, feeling it curl in his lungs like a cat on a cushion, and he felt the gentle mountain breeze caress his muscular, bare, brown arms and chest, almost like Zia's thick black hair did when they made love. He could hear the little stones skitter under Billy's hooves as the friendly goat sauntered back toward him, munching on whatever he'd found to eat.

†

When the mountain lion leaped, it saw only the goat, the goat that was chewing on a grain or a grass that had come from its owner's saddlebags. The lion did not see the man, who had turned toward the goat at the same time the lion leapt, the man who wished only to rub the narrow space between his goat's eyes and its quivering, moist nose. The lion did not see how the man's look had turned to horror when he saw the contents of the goat's mouth; the man who fell from the ledge from the force of the lion attacking the goat, and whose twisted, broken body now laid dead on the Andean valley thousands of feet below.

7

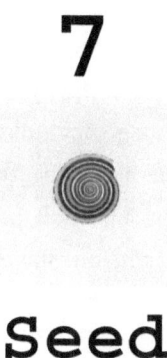

Seed

In the blood of Eden
Lie the woman and the man...
Peter Gabriel, "Blood of Eden"

The small silver cymbals tinkled pitifully, echoing mournfully from one sheer granite face to the next. The mountain lion's mouth dripped with goat's blood; its thick, gore-covered tongue licked the cool, clear water from the burst goatskin bag, water that had small, hard grains of Tuck and Zia's precious corn. The beast stretched lazily, drunk with gore, and padded away, leaving the carcass for the vultures that were already circling in the painfully bright blue sky above.

They came soon after, feasting on the leftovers Billy's death had provided. Careless in their abundance, two goat bones, still covered in blood, and to which grains of corn adhered, skidded off the cliff to a grassy plateau that Tuck's body had narrowly missed in its fall. The seeds met earth, and stayed.

Only an hour later, the vultures perched three mountains away and a few thousand feet lower. One by one, they defecated on a pristine pine struggling for existence in the high altitude. Their shit hit four pinecones ready to fall; the force caused the cones to drop onto the fertile ground below. The seeds met earth, and stayed.

It took the lion's digestive system much longer to process Billy and the precious grains, but when its bowels emptied, it was near the path to the retreat where the men of the Ouxacotl village, including their Chief, could ask favors of the Great God, who lived in the sun. The feces, with its hidden treasure of undigested grain, landed on a grassy knoll covered with an array of brightly colored flowers. The seeds met earth, and stayed.

The Chief of Ouxacotl, pleading with the Great God in the hot, hazy sun, saw the man fall from the sky. He hurried back to the village and assembled a team to help him find and properly bury the body, before wild animals had their way with it. The sun had dipped behind Tuck's mountain before they came upon the body, grotesquely draped over the craggy top of a boulder. Gently, the men brought him down as best they could. Turning him over for their older and wiser Chief to identify, one of the young men saw the half-chewed grain-cob Tuck's death grip had not surrendered. It took all the young man's strength to prise open Tuck's fingers; reverently, he handed the sad-looking stalk to Chief, who looked at it with wonder. Thoughtfully, he looked at the man on the ground, then at the stalk, then at each of the young men in turn. He held up the tiny bit of life, with its eight still-clinging grains, and smiled toward the Great God. Then he stretched forth his right arm, presenting his gift.

"Teosinte!" he shouted, his voice booming, echoing from valley to mountaintop.

"Teosinte!" chorused the young men, smiling at each other, and at Chief. They placed Tuck on the crude stretcher they had brought with them, and carried him back to the village, chanting *Teosinte* in their guttural voices.

†

Zia, pounding the corn into flour with her two stones, felt her heart turn to ice. A cold draft entered the hut, causing the pelts at the doorway to swing swiftly to and fro. She quickly got to her feet and went to look outside. "Teosinte!" she cried. The wind mocked her, echoing her beloved's name from every rock crevice.

She knew he was dead. She placed her hands on either side of the doorway to hold her up as she softly sobbed, "Teosinte! Teosinte!" Her tears glistened on her high cheekbones and full lips. A flutter, deep in her womb, caused her to quickly place her right hand on her abdomen. "Teosinte?" she whispered.

His seed had met her womb, and stayed.

8

Kids

Don't turn your back on me baby, I just might pick up my magic sticks.
Santana, "Black Magic Woman"

Ouxacotl's Chief had recognized Teosinte as the man who had been living high in the mountains with his beautiful young wife, a woman from his village. Teosinte was known by the older residents of Ouxacotl simply as "the Mountain Man." Chief, although he had never seen the farm, had a vague idea of where it might be, and now he worried for Zia's safety. He hastily called a meeting of the wise ones, sending a swift messenger to each of the eight men who made up the council, asking them to meet at the retreat.

Because it was night, no one noticed the mountain lion dung in a large pile just beside the grassy path to the lodge. They were all hurrying to the emergency meeting, and not paying attention to the sign of danger, a lion's dung, too close to the village.

Chief spoke first. "I thank you for coming together on such short notice. Today was a sad, strange day, but the Sun is all-conscious and wise."

Gray-haired heads nodded, solemnly. The elders intoned, "Praise the Wise Sun."

"Let us ask the Sun for wisdom and guidance." The nine heads lifted; nine pairs of eyes closed gently; nine pairs of hands raised, head-height, palms-out, in supplication. Chief continued, "Great Sun God, look upon us with your shining countenance. Grant us wisdom; grant us compassion; grant us pure hearts and true; grant us peace.

"We come to you this day, this day of sadness for Teosinte's wife Zia, though she knows not what has befallen her husband, unless You in Your wisdom have told her in your mysterious way.

"Teosinte's hand gripped a wild grain You, O ever-wise Sun, watched grow upon the high mountain. You have given us a gift, but we know not what to do with it.

"Zia was once of this village. Guide us; let us know if we should bring Zia home—not for greed or other unholy reason, but for her safety."

"The Sun be with us always," chanted the elders. The nine pairs of hands lowered; the nine heads straightened; the nine pairs of eyes opened. The discussion began.

†

The council decided to send two men (for they could not spare more) up the mountain to ask Zia if she would come back to the village: Javier, a young, trustworthy young man, and the Chief himself. No longer young, Chief nonetheless enjoyed excellent health and knew the ways of the mountains far better than anyone else. Although Zia might not remember him, Chief remembered her, and he knew her husband; she might feel safer going with someone she knew, someone older and wiser.

They would leave in two days, and take three goats with them, two of them with empty carrier bags to bring Zia's belongings back, as well as to provide fresh milk. It was thought wise to bring three goats, even at the risk of slowing the men down, in case something—such as a mountain lion attack—caused the death of one of the animals. It was possible that Zia would need food or milk herself; no one had visited Teosinte in the five years since he joined with Zia.

Javier and Chief set out in the pre-dawn chill of the late summer morning; all the village's residents rose early and gathered at the edge of the clearing to wish them a safe journey. Xinta, who would lead the village in Chief's absence, waved the smoldering sage stick, reserved for special occasions, solemnly over them, invoking the traveling god's blessing upon the travelers.

The men left then, and did not turn back to look at the villagers, as it was considered bad luck to do so. Another pair of eyes, however, keenly watched the unsuspecting population of Ouxacotl, standing there in the dim half-light of the approaching dawn. The lion was not yet hungry, having feasted so well on Teosinte's goat, but he would be soon. The smell of Tuck's blood still hung faintly in the air near the altar where Tuck's body had been prepared for burial. The odor could not be detected by humans, but it filled the lion's sensitive nostrils. It knew where to go for its next meal.

†

The first part of the journey was uneventful, the walk not too steep, and the sun not too hot. Javier and Chief walked in alert silence, their ears straining to catch any noise that might indicate danger—to themselves, or to the goats. Noiseless, they picked their way carefully through the forest, Javier following the elder man and observing his graceful progress.

The forest thinned and the way steepened. They stopped beside a rushing stream, getting on their haunches and drinking the ice-cold water from cupped hands. Both men soaked their long hair; it would cool them down as the climb became more strenuous. The Sun watched them from His highest point.

When night came, they had made good progress. "We are halfway to our destination," Chief said, breaking his day-long silence. "We will camp here for the night." He pointed toward a cave in front of them, its opening big enough to accommodate the two men standing up. It was not a deep cave, perhaps twenty feet, and its ceiling sloped sharply to only a few feet from the ground at its back. After herding the goats into the safety of the cave, Javier quickly built three fires, effectively creating a barrier against any wild animals that might venture by. He roasted nuts and berries for himself and Chief, and then prepared to take the first watch. The fires had to be kept alive all night, or they might all be killed in their sleep.

†

The men left at dawn the next morning. The way had become so steep there was no way to climb it without benefit of daylight. In spite of the arduous climb, Chief breathed normally; Javier followed easily behind. Around lunchtime, they came upon the place where the goat had been attacked. Chief ran his hands over the smooth rock face, looking up to the spot where the mountain lion must have perched, then he examined the becymbaled ribbon he found not two feet from the edge of the cliff. He noted the blood smears and numerous goat hairs on the wide ledge.

"Teosinte sat there," he said, pointing to the exact spot where Tuck had sat enjoying the view before his fall. "His goat came from here, and the mountain lion was there." He used first his left, then his right hand to indicate the animals' positions.

Javier nodded agreement. Chief continued, "The ribbon held his bags, one on each side of the goat." He picked up the frayed length of material and the cymbals tinkled sadly, as if they had seen too much and could bear no more. "I wonder if the grains were in the bags as well as his provisions, for why else would he venture from his home, leaving his wife alone?"

Javier surveyed the expanse of mountains beneath them. "He was coming to the village, wasn't he? He was going to share his new grain with us." Chief just placed his right hand on Javier's shoulder. "Yes."

As the orange sun dipped behind the highest mountain, Tuck's mountain, Chief and Javier heard the tinkle of goat bells before they saw the earthen home and its plume of welcoming smoke.

"Zia! Zia!" Chief called. "It is Chief from Ouxacotl, and brave young Javier, come from the village. Do not be afraid." There was no answer. "Zia!" the Chief repeated. The men waited, but the goats did not—they headed rapidly toward the area of grass beside the house.

Just as Chief and Javier started to move forward, Zia parted the doorway pelts, nearly tripping over the lintel in her haste. "Teosinte!" she cried, running toward them. She stopped abruptly when she realized her mistake. Looking anxiously at each face, her hands clasping and unclasping nervously, Zia tried to read the strangers' news. "You bring news of Teosinte?" she asked, her voice faltering.

Neither man replied; they stood in awe of Zia's beauty—face and body both. Although she had only been pregnant a short time, her breasts had become fuller, rounder; her skin glowed, both from the sun's rays and from the joy of carrying Teosinte's child. Her thick, black hair shone redly in the last of the day's sunset.

Chief was first to recover. "Zia, do you not remember me? I am Chief of your village. I blessed your union with Teosinte five years ago. You were but a girl," he smiled kindly, "but I see you are a woman now." He introduced Javier, "And this is one of Ouxacotl's strongest and kindest young men. We call him Javier." Javier smiled broadly and stood tall, but said nothing. "We would like to camp here for a few days," Chief continued, "but first there is news—"

"Teosinte is dead, isn't he." Her voice was flat, monotone. "That is what you have come to tell me," she said, her voice nearly a whisper, a strangled half-cry. She hugged herself, biting her lip to keep from crying, but tears crept silently down the high cheekbones.

Chief said simply, "Yes."

"How did he die?"

Chief told her what he thought had happened. "We have brought with us the rope of ribbon that was on your goat." He motioned to Javier, who produced the bloodstained ribbon strung with small cymbals.

Up to this point, Zia had not been overly emotional, but when she saw the ribbon, she snatched it out of Javier's hands with both of hers. Crumpling, she dropped to her knees, rocking back and forth, sobbing, touching each little cymbal in turn as if telling rosary beads. Javier started toward her, moved with compassion to try and comfort her, but Chief stayed him with a light touch on his left shoulder. Javier looked at Chief, raising his eyebrows, questioning; but Chief shook his head and put his finger to his lips as if to say, *Not now. Let her grieve.*

Their goats had wandered back, curious about the lady on the ground. One goat in particular stood near her, so close it could have kissed her. It had stopped munching, and did not even try to nibble the end of the frayed ribbon-end swinging so close to its face. It stood there, almost at attention, until Zia's tears stopped. She turned her head to look at the goat, raising her left hand to pet it. "You look like our Billy. Did you know him?" She laughed lightly. "Did you know my good man, Teosinte?" As if it understood, the goat nuzzled her neck and licked her ear.

Zia spoke then to the two men, whose faces still registered the shock of seeing one of their goats act so strangely. "Billy was the name of our goat, the one the mountain lion killed. I think he would have liked your nanny goat here very much." Turning back to the goat, she said playfully, "And I'll bet your milk is sweet, you are such a kind animal." She continued to rub the goat's face, in the long part between eyes and nose, as she said, still not quite believing it herself, "I am with child. Teosinte and I will have a son." She liked how the words felt as they came out. She repeated, a little louder, "We will have a son."

The goat knelt down beside Zia, and laid its head in her lap.

"It's time for that goat to be milked," said Chief, looking at the goat's full udder. "Would you like to milk it, Zia?"

The goat had jumped up at Chief's pronouncement and Zia laughed, saying, "It looks like maybe the goat has second thoughts!?

Tuck jumped up when he heard what Chief had said. *Holy* SHIT! *I'm a female goat? When did* that *happen?* The last thing he remembered was sitting on the ledge overlooking the valley, rubbing Billy's nose—

"Come along, little one," she said. "Let's get you milked, along with the others."

Tuck trotted along beside her, trying to digest the news that he was going to be a father. *I really shouldn't be surprised, the way we were always at it, I suppose, but after five years, who would have thought it?* His eyes were at the level of her hips; he could drink in her female smell, and was giddy from her proximity. *Now, if I can only help her decide to return with us to the village. We would have a chance to be together; I could watch over her.*

✝

After the milking, which Tuck found pleasant, if disconcerting, Zia went back to talk to Chief and Javier. "I am excited to show you something Teosinte and I were working on," she said excitedly. It is why he was going to the village, to show you."

Chief and Javier exchanged glances. "Yes, we suspected as much," said Chief. At Zia's puzzled look, he added, "There was an unfamiliar grain gripped tightly in his hand when we found him. We would be grateful," at this he bowed slightly, "if you would share your news of this grain with us."

"It is here, in this field," said Zia, pointing the way. "Follow me." Javier, Chief, and Tuck followed her. When they arrived, Tuck started, as goats do, to munch one of the stalks.

"No! You mustn't touch those grains!" She gave Tuck a stern look and swatted his behind. In spite of her harsh words, he felt aroused at her touch. *Okay, maybe she's not going to be very nice to me, but I would rather be around her than apart. She doesn't know I'm a goat, so don't blame her.* He thought of the way they had treated their animals—kindly enough, but there was still room for improvement. They were dumb animals, without souls—or so Tuck had thought until now.

Tuck left the field, but he stayed close enough to hear what they said. He also knew that Zia's beauty might be too much for those men to resist, especially Javier. *I'll do what I can to protect her.*

Meanwhile, the men inspected the grain while Zia told them of the long hours she and Teosinte had put into coaxing out the edible grains by grafting various plants on others, and waiting to see what happened. They had tried to grow it in other areas around their farm, but this sunny, southwest slope worked best.

"Come inside, and I'll show you how I make the bread. You can have some for your supper, along with the nuts and berries I've gathered here. Save your own provisions for your journey home." She turned to walk into the hut and Javier and Chief exchanged looks again, as if to say, *she doesn't know we're here to take her back with us.*

Tuck followed them as quietly as he could, hoping to sneak into the hut too, but Zia spotted him.

"You silly goat! You're not allowed in here." She looked at Javier, smiling. "Do you allow animals in the house in Ouxacotl these days, Javier?" He smiled shyly, dropping his eyes and mumbling, "No, Zia."

Oh, he's the one to watch! Tuck stomped the ground furiously, angry that he could not keep an eye on Zia, and jealous of Javier. There was nothing he could do but wait until they returned, although he might be able to hear a thing or two if he—

"What is that goat doing outside the doorway?" Tuck could hear Zia's exasperated voice. "Javier, will you use a stick and shoo her back to where the rest of the goats are, behind the house?"

Tuck didn't wait to be poked at by Javier—he hightailed it around the back of the house before Javier had a chance to get him. After a few minutes, he went to where the strangers had their belongings, wrapped up neatly in pelts—bundles he, as a goat, must have helped carry up the tortuous mountain path. He spotted Javier's bundle, selected the spot that would do the most damage, and then very carefully peed into that exact spot.

Then he calmly walked back up past the house and joined the rest of the goats, who were munching away happily on the precious grains in the field, although he didn't eat any himself.

†

It took what seemed like forever to Tuck, anxiously waiting, but finally the visitors and Zia left the hut. When he had found he could not persuade the other goats to stop ruining the crop, Tuck had trotted away. He stood apart— not quite in the field, yet not quite in front of the hut. When Zia saw the herd in the field, she sprinted toward them, the men following her, and all of them shouting, "Shoo! Shoo!" The goats scattered, but the damage was done.

"I'll bet I know which goat started this," she muttered under her breath as she inspected the break in the makeshift fence around the field. "I'm sorry, Chief, but I think that goat you brought with you, the one who laid its head in my lap, is the one who did this. Remember how it followed us into the field and started eating?" She scanned the area, looking for Tuck. "My goats would not do such a thing; they've been trained not to enter this field."

The fury that burned in Zia's eyes caused Chief to try to calm her down; she looked capable of roasting the best milk goat he owned. He walked over to one of the damaged stalks. "Although there is much damage to the grain in this section, I don't think the whole crop is ruined." He walked to another section. "See? The goats did not get this far, and these stalks are untouched."

He held up an undamaged one for her to look at. "It would be unwise to kill a goat because it did what came naturally. What if we did that to humans?"

Chagrined, Zia apologized. "You are right, Chief. The whole crop is not destroyed, and there is no need to kill the goat." She flashed him one of her smiles. "How did you know I wanted to kill that goat?"

"I could see that fire in your eyes, and knew the goat was in trouble." Chief smiled in return. "I'm sorry, but I cannot let even a beautiful woman like you kill our best milker." He moved closer, touching her lightly on her elbow. He said, with his voice lowered, "You have developed into a fine, brave woman, Zia. But are you so brave as to stay by yourself up here in this aloof spot?" He edged in a little more. "Would it not be a good idea to come back with Javier and me to live in the village?" His left arm went around the back of her shoulders, and he swept his right arm across the view, taking in the field and the mountains before them. "We know you do not want to leave this beautiful place—who would? You want to carry on for Teosinte." He gestured toward her slightly swollen belly. "And think of the baby, Zia. The women in the village will help you raise the child to be as strong and as brave as your husband." He looked over at Javier, who had a slightly perplexed look on his face. He had been inspecting the grains until he had heard Chief ask Zia to return with them to Ouxacotl; then he had walked over to learn from Chief the art of persuasion.

Tuck was coming around the corner of the hut when he saw Chief's arm around Zia's shoulders. He didn't notice the gray hair on the usurper's head; he charged. In full fury, he leapt the broken fence—which slowed him down only slightly—and butted Chief with all his might, knocking him to the ground. Javier had seen the goat coming and had moved to one side, out of the way. There was the faintest hint of a smile on his handsome face.

"*Now* can I kill the goat?" Zia looked at Tuck with pure hatred in her eyes.

This is not what I wanted. What does she mean, 'Kill the goat'? He tried willing all the love in his heart to show in his eyes, begging her to see that it was *him*, the love of her life.

Tuck saw something flicker in her eyes, a recognition—fleeting—and she gasped just a little, stretching her hand toward him. He started toward her, gaily, but was stopped cold in his tracks by Chief's next words. Tuck had not noticed the recognition in Chief's eyes, a knowledge that caused him to say, "Yes. Kill the goat." His eyes had narrowed to malevolent slits. "It will do us *all* good to have some fresh meat around here."

†

Zia could do nothing to stop it. Chief slaughtered the goat himself, while a reluctant Javier built a great outdoor fire and spit, upon which he placed the goat. Zia was allowed to make the special bread using the indoor fire, and she stayed there, pounding and pounding the grain to microscopic bits, for as long as she could. Eventually, though, she had to join Chief and Javier outside for the meal.

"Here," said Chief, 'you must take the first bite. You are the one who wanted to kill the goat in the first place; you have earned this first piece." Zia began to take it from his hand, tears streaming down her face, but she jumped up instead, putting her hand over her mouth, then running toward the hut. She didn't make it inside, and vomited near its front doorway.

Javier, torn between loyalty to his Chief and compassion for the woman, started to rise and go after Zia, but Chief ordered, "Sit down. She vomits because she is pregnant, and not for any other reason. There is no need to go to her." Chief continued to relish the roasted meat, its juices running down his chin and onto the elaborate loincloth he wore. "Now eat. We need our strength for the journey. We travel back to the village tomorrow." Javier sat cross-legged again, picked up some of the meat, and choked it down as best he could.

†

That night Zia packed the few belongings she had, placing the worn, blood-marked ribbon in with the jewelry Teosinte had made for her. She held the small pouch between her breasts, saying softly, "Forgive me for my folly today, my love. You are with me always, like the Sun, my Teosinte. And I am with you." She looped the pouch strings over and around her waist belt in such a way that with every right-footed step, she would feel its weight upon her thigh. Then she curled up on her mat and slept, peacefully, quite resigned to her fate.

It seemed only an hour or two later when she was awakened by someone kneeling on her mat, close beside her. "Is it time already?" she mumbled sleepily. "How quickly the time went. I feel as if I've only laid down a moment ago." She rolled over, intending to rise, but stopped when she saw Chief beside her, on his knees.

Roughly, he pushed her back upon the mat, saying, "Lie down and open yourself to me." She opened her mouth to scream for Javier, but Chief quickly clapped his huge hand over her small mouth. "*Don't...make... a... sound...*" he grunted, forcing himself into her as she squirmed in vain, trying to get away, "*...or—I—will—kill—you.*"

With every thrust of his powerful loins, Zia felt the little leather pouch brush her leg, and she cried silent, bitter tears.

†

She prepared, in utter silence, to leave the next morning. Javier noted the way Chief treated Zia—coming up behind her, trying to help her tie the provisions to the goats' backs, gently brushing her shoulders when he passed by. He saw Zia shudder when Chief did these things; he saw her run toward the house and vomit as she had the night before. Javier, a smart as well as a handsome young man, now realized where Chief had gone in the middle of the night when he thought Javier was asleep. He also knew there was nothing he could do; as Chief, he was entitled to have his choice of women.

The packing was done; they left the mountain. Zia turned, only once, to bid a sad, silent farewell to the home that for her had held such love. All the goats trotted along happily behind, oblivious to the tragedy of the night before.

The journey was long, but uneventful. Chief did not molest Zia again, because of Javier's proximity, but he did try to fondle her when he thought Javier wasn't looking. Javier showed Zia the spot where Billy had been attacked by the mountain lion, and Tuck had fallen; both men allowed her to sit by herself and grieve there before moving on.

An eerie sound, a keening sound, wafted in the sunset's haze toward them as they reached the outskirts of the village on the third evening. Concerned that no one was there to greet them—guards should have been alerted to their coming at least a half hour ago—Chief and Javier ran ahead, leaving Zia to walk, with the goats, into the near-silent place which would now be her home.

It was just as well the men had gone on ahead: the appalling scene that greeted them caused Javier to retch like Zia had done up on the mountain. While they were away, the mountain lion had come for his dinner—and brought his own family with him. They had attacked the villagers without mercy, leaving half-eaten bodies which had rotted quickly in the summer's heat. Vultures had, of course, picked on the carrion remaining; Chief and Javier had tried to frighten them away before Zia came to the spot. It was as if the birds knew they were in no danger—what were two men going to do against a hundred vultures?

Javier ran back to where Zia was struggling along the path, exhausted, thirsty, and dry-heaving at the stench that was almost palpable. "Don't come any closer, Zia!" he warned. "There has been a terrible tragedy in Ouxacotl— lions have attacked the village and there is death all around." His strong young hands were surprisingly gentle on her shoulders as he kept her from going forward. "I'm so sorry, Zia," he faltered, his compassion for her situation nearly overwhelming him, "for... for... everything." Zia collapsed into his arms, sobbing.

9

Sand

This way she moves, in the logic of all my dreams
This fire burns; I realize that nothing's as it seems.
Sting, "Desert Rose"

Tuck woke up, his mouth sandy and gritty. *Was I drinking last night?* He breathed on the back of his hand to see if he smelled like alcohol. *Hmm. Besides morning breath, seems okay. So what's with the grit in my teeth?* He looked around him—he seemed to be in some sort of tent, an elegant one. It was bright and airy, but extremely hot inside. *Could it be any hotter? It feels like an oven. Maybe I'm in Vegas. Somehow I don't think so, though.* He checked out what he was wearing: white, billowy cotton of the finest grade—*Egyptian?*—which had been made into wide-legged trousers; a sort of long vest, beautifully embroidered in what looked like silver thread; long-sleeved shirt, high-collared, huge sleeves, really airy, and also made from the light, white cotton. *If I've got a turban, I think I know where I am.* He put his hands up to his head. *No turban! But wow, my hair is wiry and thick.* He looked to his left, to a low stool on which more clothing was piled. *Okay, maybe I don't have a turban, but here's the headgear.* He picked up the small, round, white hat that stood about three inches high, and was also embroidered in silver. He tried placing it on his head, but it toppled off. *Must be a trick to putting it on.* He bent to pick it up, whirling it on his fist like it was pizza dough. *What's this called again? It's not a yarmulke, but it's sorta like that.*

It appeared he had the tent to himself, large as it was. Apparently he'd been here for a while, as there were signs of several days' clothing erupting out of leather-bound trunks, as well as meal leftovers. *I am so thirsty. What's to drink around here?* He couldn't get rid of the sandy grit in his mouth. *Guess it's time to find out where I really am, and if there's any water to drink. Oh, a cup of coffee would be nice right now!*

He got up and went to the door of the tent, unzipping it rapidly. *Well, here goes.* He stepped out into the brightest sunlight he'd ever encountered. *Jeesus! Where are my sunglasses?* He ducked back inside the tent. On the other side of the makeshift bed laid a pair of sunglasses. He went over to pick them up. *Hmm. Nice. They look like—geez, they are!—Ray-Bans. I must be traveling in style this time.* He put them on and went outside again.

Yes, it was unbearably hot. But it was also incredibly beautiful, in its own way. Reddish-gold dunes of sparkling sand stretched in every direction, except to his right, where palm trees surrounded a tiny, pristine lake. There were three other tents, one much larger, the other two the same size as his, nearby; there were also ATVs, and three Mercedes SUVs with trailers. From the direction of the lake, he could now hear the sounds of people splashing and laughing, the constant, low wind having shifted so the sounds drifted toward him.

He wandered over to the water, which was about a hundred yards from the tents. *I wonder why they don't park nearer?* As he got closer, those in the water and on the shore began waving and shouting. "Akhi!" "Khali!" *They're saying 'Brother' and 'Uncle'—and I can understand them!* Tuck watched them play, understanding them.

"Look at me!" "Watch me jump!" A child, about twelve, did a cannonball from a small portable, inflatable, dock. "What took you so long? You are missing all the fun!"

Tuck waved and smiled, walking toward them and shouting back answers. *I'm speaking Arabic!* Somehow, he not only understood what they were shouting at him, but he understood himself, speaking this strange tongue with ease. *I'm not sure when I picked this up, but I'm glad I did. Let's see if I can get something to drink—and something to eat would be great, too.*

"Hello everyone!" Tuck shouted.

"We thought you were never going to get up, Aziz. Why did you stay in bed so long? We've only got three days here, and you're spending it sleeping—that's crazy!" Tuck thought it might be his brother who spoke to him like this, but he wasn't sure, not yet.

"So, what's to eat?" asked Tuck. "And where's the water?" They all laughed at him; Tuck had no idea why. He noticed they didn't have any food—or drinks, for that matter—around them either. *Okay, what's up here? I'm missing something.* The tallest of the three men sitting beside the lake nudged the shortest one, who was sitting next to him.

"Sulaiman, listen to him. Our brother is a comedian." Both men laughed, and Sulaiman said, "He's always been the silliest of us all, Abdullah." Turning to the other man, he said, "What do you think, Mohamad? You're the psychiatrist. Is our brother crazy?"

Mohamad tried to keep a straight face as he said, "If this man were to enter my office, almost three weeks after Ramadan had started, asking for food and water, I would think he had either just come out of a coma or he was visiting from another planet." He looked Tuck up and down. "Actually, I think he *might* be an alien." The men all laughed, but none harder than Tuck. *If they only knew!*

Just then Tuck was nearly knocked over by a small, wet body who threw his arms around Tuck's knees and said, "Uncle! Uncle! I am so so so happy you decided to wake up! You must come and watch me swim!" The skinny little boy ran and did a cannonball into the lake.

"That's not swimming, that's splashing," Tuck yelled. "You should let me show you how to do it!" He started taking off his clothes, but the other men gasped loudly enough for him to turn and look at them, questioning, "What? Why not? I'm a champion swimmer, after all." *What are we doing at a lake if we can't swim?* Tuck thought, exasperated. First no water, then no food—now this.

Mohamad said, "Lads, I think your brother really *is* an alien. Either that, or he's suffering from amnesia." The men were now looking at Tuck with alarm; they were no longer laughing.

Sulaiman said, as if he were explaining something to a child, "Water might enter your mouth if you swim." *Ah…isn't that the point? I'm parched here.* "And have you forgotten that the women are with us? They're nearby, and could come out here at any time." He shook his head. "Really, Aziz, sometimes you go too far with your jokes. It's bad enough you missed prayer time earlier, but to swim is unacceptable, and you know that. Not during Ramadan."

Tuck gulped with what little spit he had. "*Smahne*, my brothers; Mohamad. I did forget myself, and I apologize." *Geez, what am I going to do here? This is crazy! What do I know about Ramadan, for chrissake. Or Islam, for that matter. One thing is sure, though, I must be the black sheep of this family.* Tuck stood there, unsure of what to do next.

Tuck saw the looks on the men's faces change, and even the children in the lake became quieter. The men were staring, almost gawping, at something or someone behind him. Turning slowly on his heel in the hot sand, he saw three women approach. Correction, three *stunning* women, approach the shady spot in which the men sat. The most beautiful of them all was in the lead, the other two trailing her slightly. Each of them wore a rich-hued *matasharba*, which complemented her gauzy, flowing trousers and blouse. Each wore a brilliant white smile as well.

Tuck stood, dumbstruck. He didn't know if he should kneel or not, but he wanted to in the face of such beauty. He heard the men behind him rise to their feet, then one of them—Sulaiman?—call out their names: "Zia! Mosliya! Lutfia! You've come to join us!"

"Ah, my Aziz!" the leading one, the most beautiful one, cried, running toward Tuck and enveloping him in a warm hug, kissing him soundly on both cheeks. *My Zia!* Tuck was sure he had reached heaven. *I don't care if I ever eat again. With Zia as my wife, I think I can live without food and water forever.* He wanted to kiss her passionately right there, but he sensed that Ramadan rules might have something to say about that kind of thing, too. He brought all his love and passion up to his eyes, letting them do his talking for him. Zia's smile, upon seeing this welling of passion in Tuck's eyes, faltered a little. She dropped her arms quickly, and backed up. Tuck noticed that the other women did not come to give him a hug, although they greeted him, and the other men, warmly enough.

The women joined them, laughing and joking too, and Tuck tried to figure out who went with who. From what he gathered, Sulaiman's wife was Lutfia, and Abdullah's wife was Mosliya. It was difficult to tell, as none of them wore wedding rings; each man was kissed the same way—on both cheeks—by each woman, so that was no help, either. He did figure out, though, that the skinny child who had left a wet ring around the knees of Tuck's billowy trousers was Lutfia's. The two older children seemed to be Mohamad's, but maybe his wife wasn't here. None of the women looked old enough to have teenagers. *Things are looking good! Zia must be my wife. No wonder I slept late.*

Tuck sat on the ground, his knees wrapped in his arms, and just listened to the happy babble of voices around him—that is, when he wasn't staring at Zia. He felt like an idiot around her. She was so beautiful, and (probably) all his!

Tuck gathered from what the men were saying that the women had been making food for the "break of fast," which would be in an hour or two. The sun lowered slowly, lazily, tingeing the surrounding dunes with gold, orange, and red hues in a way Tuck had never seen before, or at least, not noticed before. *I really did sleep late. No wonder they thought I was crazy.* What he couldn't believe was how much laughter there was, when no one had had anything to eat all day. The men had, of course, told the women about Tuck's food and water requests, and Tuck had had to endure a further round of ribbing. From their conversations, he figured out that they went without food and water from sunup to sundown. For a whole month, no less! *And they think I'm crazy.*

When only an inch of the orange sun was left in the sky, the women went back to what must have been the food tent, while the men waited for them to return and serve them. The men's main job was to spread a gigantic tablecloth on the ground for everyone to sit around. Then the food started to arrive: couscous, three kinds of chicken, grape leaves stuffed with rice, spiced potatoes. These were the ones Tuck recognized; there was such an abundance of food he couldn't believe it. *It's like Thanksgiving, but they do it every night for a month. They may not eat anything in the daytime, but they sure make up for it at night.* There was no alcohol, but there were all sorts of juices and, finally, water.

Before they could eat, however, there was a solemn story told, and a prayer said. Everyone listened, rapt, as Mohamad read from the Qur'ân and told them the story of Ramadan. Tuck found himself drawn into the story in spite of himself. He was even able to stop staring at Zia.

When Mohamad finished, the feast began. It took them hours to finish—they all ate slowly, talking and laughing between each morsel. As he got full, Tuck started thinking about what the night would bring; that he would be with Zia again. As if she read his thoughts, she looked over at him, giving him her special smile. *She's sitting beside Mohamad, but that's probably because she was serving the food.* Mohamad had been tonight's Ramadan speaker.

It was nearly one o'clock in the morning when the adults prepared to retire to their tents, the children having gone to bed earlier. The women left for their own tent, while each man had his own to go to. "Zia," Tuck said, "aren't you coming with me?" Sulaiman and Abdullah stopped in their tracks, turning to face Tuck, while Mohamad went on ahead to his own tent.

"Do you want Zia to tuck you in, brother?" Sulaiman joked. "Aren't you a little old for that?"

"Ah, leave him alone." Abdullah laughed. "He's our little brother, after all. Our little alien!" The two men, chuckling, continued on to their tents.

Zia, who had been leaving with the other women, stopped uncertainly. "You need me, Aziz?" she asked. When he nodded, she said, over her shoulder, "Mosliya. . . Lutfia. . . I will catch up with you in a moment. I must go with Aziz." They nodded and waved, calling good night in the cool night air.

Zia and Tuck walked toward his tent, Zia being the first to break the silence. "You have been acting strangely today, Aziz. Especially the way you've been looking at me." She paused outside the door to his tent. "Is everything all right?"

"Of course it is!" said Tuck, surprised. He held open the tent flap, "Come in, come in." She hesitated. "What is there to be afraid of? Come in, Zia, for god's sake." Almost gingerly, she stepped through into his tent.

"I see you are as messy as ever, Aziz," she said, taking in the chaotic scene around her. "I did not know you had brought so much with you. You could nearly live out here!" She turned to face him, giggling. "Is that why you brought me here? To tidy up, Aziz?" She took off her *hijab* and smoothed back her glistening black hair. "It's so warm in here, Aziz!" She undid the two top buttons of her linen blouse. "It's too late to clean up your mess, and I'm bushed. I'm going back to my tent." She turned away slightly, but his hand shot out and grabbed her by the shoulder.

"You know why I brought you here," Tuck said thickly. "How could you not know? Ramadan or not, I must have you." He embraced her, trying to kiss her, but she squirmed and tried to escape his arms. Tuck was baffled, but so aroused he was unable to stop himself.

"What are you doing! Stop! Aziz!" Her voice, though low, was urgent, pained. "Stop!"

"I saw how you looked at me. You want me, too, I know it! Why are you trying to get away?! Zia!" She had broken away, though he still had her right arm and was gripping it tightly, bruising her, pulling her back to him. Her *hajib* fell to the ground, and she bent to pick it up.

"No!" She was sobbing now. Just then, a figure came through the door of the tent. It was Mohamad, and he stood, his arms crossed, blocking Zia's exit. His eyes took in the scene before him: Aziz's shocked face; Zia, her blouse undone and her *hajib* in her hand, on her knees in front of Aziz; Aziz's hand still gripping her shoulder as if he were pushing her to the ground. Mohamad could not make out the tears on Zia's face because of the angry mist in his own eyes. He folded his arms menacingly across his broad chest.

"What," growled Mohamad, "are you doing with *my wife?*"

Neither Tuck nor Zia anticipated Mohamad's next move. The aggrieved husband's right hand shot out, slapping Zia so hard in the face that she was knocked on her side. "And Zia, you slut." He spat on the ground. "*What* have you done with *your brother?*"

Tuck, revolted by what he had almost done with his sister had Mohamad had not come through the door when he did, ran out of the tent and vomited outside its opening. Mohamad read Tuck's reaction as proof of Zia's wrongdoing. "There! You see what your brother thinks of your actions!" Tuck could hear him slap Zia again and again.

Tuck staggered back into the tent. "No! No! Mohamad, it was not Zia's fault! I am the—"

Mohamad stopped him cold, his hand, held up like a policeman's, preventing him from uttering another syllable. "I know you want to take the blame so your sister will not die, but I cannot let you do that." He looked at her, then spat on the ground, violently, again. "She will get the punishment she deserves. This holiday is over. We leave immediately."

Zia's eyes, filled with tears, looked at Tuck with total incomprehension. Mohamad dragged her out, half-kneeling, into the cool, starry night.

†

A somber group headed back to Riyadh a few hours later, after packing in total darkness, and leaving as the morning's light broke on the seas of sand around them. No questions were asked of Tuck; indeed, his brothers tried to console him, each placing a hand on one of his shoulders, their eyes bright with unshed tears. Tuck's tears were misunderstood.

They arrived in Riyadh as the first of the "Little Lamb Lots" opened for business, selling the lambs used for tithing, a payment to be shared among the poor and less fortunate of the city. Zia's trial was set for September 8, the week after Ramadan ended.

Tuck, in the courtroom, could do nothing for her; helpless, he heard the verdict: immediate death by stoning. The outside world's media, because they were not allowed to cover the actual stoning, did not witness Tuck as he hurled stones at Zia, an act in which he was required to perform, as were the rest of his family and, of course, Mohamad. After her death, after seeing his beloved Zia buried under the pile of stones stained with her blood, the media vultures waited for Tuck. He was unwilling to answer any of their questions; this was interpreted, worldwide, as Tuck's agreement with Zia's punishment. Because of his refusal to give them any juicy sound bites, the disappointed reporters let him leave with his family; they dropped him off at the front door of his spacious home.

Once inside its front doors, Tuck went into the mahogany-lined library, with its hundreds of leather-bound books. He opened the top right-hand drawer of his enormous desk. Then he took out a gun, one he had bought two days ago while his brothers thought he was getting a haircut, and which he had loaded before he went to Zia's stoning.

After saying a short prayer asking Allah's forgiveness, he said, quietly, "I love you, Zia." He then placed the gun snug against his right temple, closed his eyes, and shot himself.

10

Absolution

Between the two of us guys, you know I love you more
It took me by surprise, I must say, when I found out yesterday.

Marvin Gaye, "Heard It Through the Grapevine"

Half-waking, Tuck threw his right arm over the warm body beside him. He snuggled in, burying his face into the thick, black, long hair—nearly waist-length—and bending his knees so they would fit perfectly into hers. He nuzzled and kissed her neck through the thick hair that smelled of almonds, and felt himself grow hard with desire. "Mmm. Wake up, Zia," he murmured thickly. "Come to daddy." He felt an answering stir in the naked slim hips and tight buttocks that touched his skin. His hand slipped down to what should have been her voluptuous breasts, but they weren't there. In his half-asleep state, he didn't notice this, however. He just pulled her even closer, his fumbling fingers still trying to find the missing breasts. He searched lower, trying to get to the part he knew would still be there. His hand gently moved, lower…lower…

She turned toward him, kissing him passionately, as if she would like to swallow him whole. Her mustache tickled his upper lip—

Tuck bolted upright in bed, fumbling for the light, panic-stricken, only there didn't seem to be a bedside light, only unlit candles, candles, and more candles, some of which had tumbled to the floor.

Please let this be a dream. His partner had not stopped fondling him—had, in fact, begun fellating him in an expert manner. Tuck was aroused intensely in spite of himself. As his eyes adjusted to the dimness, he could see that in the corners of the room stood several large candles on stands, although none of them were close enough for him to light. Tuck could see well enough to make out the body so intimate now with his own. He parted the hair, so like Zia's, that had fallen like a curtain over him, and the person—he wasn't ready to admit it was a man—expertly giving him the best oral gratification of his life. He didn't need to look, really. He could feel the mustache brushing his skin. It wasn't Zia: it was a man. Tuck verified that first; then he fainted.

†

Tuck felt someone shaking him violently, bringing him back to the awful present. "No, no—"

A hand clamped over his mouth, and Tuck opened his eyes in spite of his nearly overwhelming desire not to. *Please let this be a dream. Please.* The beautiful, mustached face had eyes full of tears, and the owner of the face was shaking his head back and forth, putting the index finger of his free hand on his lips, pleading with his eyes for Tuck not to say anything or to make any noise. Tuck nodded that he understood he had to be quiet, and the lover took his hand away from Tuck's mouth. He let him lie there, still unaware of Tuck's revulsion. He tenderly touched Tuck's face, stroking it gently, gave him small hugs, as if Tuck were fragile and would break if he hugged him any harder.

After a final embrace, the man eased himself from the bed and began dressing, hurriedly putting on strange-looking, coarse, long underwear, then a sort of rough cotton vest. Tuck's eyes widened when the man slipped into a monk's robes, and tied a thick white rope around his waist.

Tuck darted glances around the candlelit room, taking in the dozens of beeswax candles in various sizes; the large wooden cross on the wall; the painting of the sacred heart of Jesus; the rough stone floor, the narrow bed which had barely fit the two men. And he saw, hung up carefully on a makeshift hook on the arched planked door, what must be his own robe. It looked like it might be made of finer stuff than that worn by the beautiful man beside him, who was now brushing Tuck's hair using short, rhythmic strokes.

Instinctively, Tuck reached up and felt the top of his head. It was not covered luxuriously like the other man's; Tuck's had a huge bald spot. *I've got a tonsure! What in god's name have I done now? Holy shit, I must be a priest. A fucking priest.* Tuck had never been religious, or at least not in that long-ago lifetime he could still recall, the one before his twenty-fifth anniversary and that crazy movie theater. His parents had given him the choice of whether to go to church or not, and he decided "not." *And now I'm sleeping with young men. Well, at least I'm not a very good priest, that's some comfort.* His lover took Tuck's hands in both of his, squeezing them tightly, then kissing each fingertip. He leaned over and kissed Tuck full on the mouth, tenderly.

"Can yo—"

The young man's eyes, big and dark, look terrified, as if he couldn't believe Tuck would venture to say anything. His lover shook his head violently again, only stopping when he heard a bell toll, sonorous and deep, intoning the hour. He rose.

This must be his cue to leave. The young man went to Tuck's door, inched it open, furtively looked out, and then, with a final small wave and a blown kiss, slipped out the door, probably to his own room. If the bells were anything to go by, it was three o'clock in the morning. Tuck, however, was getting no more sleep that night, no matter how early (or late) it might be.

He heard the bells toll four, and then five o'clock. He began to hear shuffling noises in the hall outside his room; then he heard a lighter, higher bell, after which a similarly tonsured man knocked lightly and popped his head in. He seemed dismayed that Tuck was still naked. He made motions which Tuck interpreted to mean: *Get up! Get your clothes on! Time to eat!* The gestures for these were fairly easy to understand, although his motions for "Have you lost your mind?" were a little more difficult to fathom. The monk left the room then, but not before he'd seen Tuck hop out of bed, buck naked. Tuck thought he saw a little raise of the eyebrows and a *Hmm—not bad, not bad at all!* look in the monk's eyes. *Jeez, I wonder if I've slept with that guy too.* Miserably, Tuck put on his clothes, wondering what was in store for him beyond that wooden door.

He walked out, his bare feet freezing on the cold stone floor. He hadn't been able to find any shoes, but by the look of things, no one else wore them either. As he went down the hall, he couldn't help but admire the stone architecture; the wall sconces set in deep recesses; the entire hallway arched and echoey. *It's like a castle. I wonder how big this place is? Must be a devil to keep heated.* Shivering, he had no more time to wonder—a larger door than that to his bedroom loomed before him. He grabbed its wrought iron handle and it opened easily.

There, in a long, low-ceilinged, wide room were more than a dozen trestle tables, each seating at least ten monks. He didn't see his visitor from the night before, but then, these monks all had their clothes on. The monks were not yet seated. No, they were standing; and they were all looking at Tuck. *Christ, they're waiting for* me! *Shit!* The monk who had popped his head into Tuck's room earlier came forward from one of the front tables, rolling his eyes. He led Tuck to the top table, where a wonderful breakfast awaited him. Just as he was going to sit down, Tuck felt the monks' two hundred-or-so eyes upon him. Praying he was doing the right thing, he made a huge sign of the cross which he hoped covered everyone, and then he bowed his head, motioning for the monks to sit down. The Eye-Roller came forward again, pointing to the small brass bell on Tuck's table, as if to say, *Ring it, stupid! Let's eat before this wonderful meal is frozen solid.* Tuck, keeping his eyes on that monk, tentatively rang the bell. To his—and everyone's—relief, they all sat down and started eating.

They're not saying *anything. This could be a good thing.* Tuck tried to think through his new situation as he slurped down the thin but tasty porridge, and ate the fresh, thick bread spread with honey. *A nice big cup of coffee would go perfectly with this. I wonder what's in this cup?* To his delight, it was wine—not too sweet, not too dry, something he'd never had before. *Woo-hoo! This is breakfast, right? I wonder what they drink at supper? They probably make this stuff themselves, lots of those monks do. I could get to like this very much.* Tuck ate with gusto, grateful he didn't have to say anything, ring any bells, or sleep with any men—at least for the time being.

It was after they had finished eating that Tuck saw his nighttime visitor again. His long hair was tied back into a long ponytail, and he kept his eyes lowered respectfully. He was part of the kitchen staff, apparently, because he was clearing away the dishes as each monk finished his meal. He didn't have a tonsure, either, so he must not have taken holy orders yet. When he came to Tuck's table, Tuck tried to catch his eye, but the young man gave no sign he knew Tuck at all. As he cleared the dishes away, however, he brushed Tuck's fingers twice, lingering for the fraction of a second it took Tuck to realize that the young man was communicating as best he could under the circumstances. As Tuck watched him glide from table to table, he couldn't help but think he had seen that walk before; that gliding, almost dancing movement, with slim waist and mobile hips.

Just as he recognized Zia's walk, the young man turned and looked Tuck straight in the eye. He smiled—oh-so-quickly, oh-so-subtly—and Tuck smiled back. Neither man realized that the Eye-Roller, too, had seen this exchange; the lovers were too wrapped up in their own world.

Tuck took one last sip of wine, and then followed the other monks down another long hallway, which opened, not surprisingly, into a splendid, though small, cathedral. There were twelve stained-glass windows depicting the stations of the cross, and an altar carved from marble, surrounded by dozens and dozens of candles and bedecked with flowers—lupins, lilies-of-the-valley, heather, violets. The mesmerizing smell of incense, together with the wine he'd had at breakfast, and his lack of sleep, caused Tuck to doze briefly, even sitting there on the unforgiving pews. When everyone rose—at the sound of yet another bell—it woke Tuck up. He was relieved to discover no one expected him to lead mass. *Boy, would they be in for a surprise!* Lucky for Tuck, he was a member of a silent order and, at least this morning, it seemed to be an "each-monk-for-himself" arrangement.

The monks knelt in unison when the next bell sounded. There were no cushioned kneeling rails like in the churches Tuck remembered; no, the other monks, silent, unperturbed, all knelt on the cold stone floor. *This is going to kill me! How long are we going to do this?* Tuck's kneecaps screamed for relief. He bowed his head with the rest, willing himself not to cry out in pain, fall over, or worse—snore. He was so tired, he thought he might just fall asleep in spite of the pain he felt.

He was getting used to the dull ache when he felt an urgent tap on his right shoulder. Starting, he saw Eye-Roller tugging at his sleeve, motioning him to come along with him. *Gladly! Anything to get off this stone floor.* His feet had gone numb from kneeling, causing him to stumble as he rose. The pins-and-needles feeling nearly caused him to cry out, it was so intense, but he managed to keep it in, following Eye–Roller out a smaller door at the rear of the chapel, and down yet another hallway, this one darker and less used, if the dust and cobwebs were anything to go by.

Eye-Roller stopped, turned to face Tuck, and with his right hand, gestured him through an open door into a small room. Eye-Roller remained outside, pulling the door shut after he let Tuck in. There, in front of him, Tuck saw his nighttime visitor—his Zia—with his back to him, stripped to the waist, hands manacled to the wall. There were large, bloody marks down his back, and he was crying softly. From another door to the right of this scene walked another man in clerical dress, but different from either Tuck or Zia. He carried an evil-looking whip of braided leather in his right hand, tapping it on his left palm as he walked, looking for Tuck's reaction to the scene.

"Do you know this man?" asked the man with the whip, who pointed to Zia. Zia looked back at Tuck, begging with his eyes not to acknowledge their relationship.

But Tuck could not bear to see Zia tortured like this for his sake; man or woman, this was his Zia, and he loved him. "Yes. Yes, I do." Gratitude shone in Zia's eyes as he spoke. "As a matter of fact, I love him."

Whip-Monk was surprised at Tuck's confession; he looked almost disappointed: this would be too easy. "You acknowledge that you know this man?"

"Yes."

Incredulous, the man asked, "Do you deny having sexual relations with this man, in direct contravention of Church law?"

"I do not deny it." Zia looked at him, his eyes a mix of love and terror. "I love this man," Tuck repeated.

"Then you know you must hang for your crime." He paused a moment before saying, "And you will both be tortured, first, by whipping, then on the rack."

Tuck gave Zia a long look, full of love, before speaking. "I understand. I ask only that the two of us hang from the same scaffold."

†

After three days of torture, Tuck and Zia, barely able to stand, were brought to the scaffold. Eye-Roller, Whip-Monk, and the rest of the monks and apprentices were assembled around them; the Church did not want to miss an opportunity to warn others of the dangers of homosexual behavior. Tuck and Zia, each wearing a rope around his neck, stood next to each other on the platform. Just before the bottom dropped from under them, each reached for the other's hand, holding tightly until life was snapped away from them both.

11

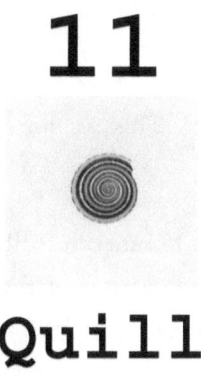

Quill

Moses was a juggler. Jesus was an acrobat and his mother a whore.
Christopher Marlowe

His cramped, cold fingers gripped, with his left hand, a quill pen that was in need of more ink. Tuck looked: first, at his writing hand (he'd never been left-handed before); second, down at the page he must have been working on.

> ~~Oh Helena, launcher of a thousand~~
>
> ~~Oh Helen, whose thousand ships~~
>
> *Dear Helena, whose thousand ships should—*

Tuck thought he recognized the lines, though he couldn't remember who'd written them offhand. *Shakespeare? Who was that one guy Zia liked so much...Marlowe, I think it was.* Tuck looked at the lines again. They didn't look quite right... *Let's see. I think they go more like this....* He dipped the quill into the nearby ink jar, and wrote:

> *Was this the face that launch'd a thousand ships*
> *And burnt the topless towers of Ilium?*
> *Sweet Helen, make me immortal with a kiss.*

Her lips suck forth my soul: see where it flies!
Come, Helen, come, give me my soul again.
Here will I dwell, for heaven is in these lips,
And all is dross that is not Helena.

Tuck set the quill pen in its brass holder, then rubbed his hands together gleefully. "Oh yes! Much better. This writing thing's easy, as long as you've already seen the script—"

"What script?" A voice boomed into the high-ceilinged room, a room Tuck noticed was full of books—on top of the table, the two chairs, the two single beds in opposite corners. *Plenty of drink bottles, too.* He turned to stare at the young man who had blustered into the room, who was unknotting and flinging aside the white scarf trailing from his thin neck. "*Don't* tell me you've finished that dreadful *Faustus* and the King's Men are going to pro*duce* it?"

Faustus! thought Tuck. That's the name of the play, *The Tragicall History of the Life and Death of Doctor Faustus.* Tuck inwardly gave himself a pat on the back. *Must've learned something from Zia after all. She was always going on about Marlowe, back in the*—. He'd almost finished his thought with: future.

The other man had proceeded to take off his woolen greatcoat, which Tuck noticed was frayed at its hems, both bottom and cuff. The white puffy shirt tucked into the man's black breeches was no longer very white, and showed worse wear than the greatcoat. He kicked off his nearly heel-less shoes and flopped onto the faded, brocaded settee along the wall opposite the desk at which Tuck sat. Tuck saw the holes in the socks that needed darning—and couldn't help but recoil at the smell of feet that had been in leather shoes alternately soaked in rain and dried by a pub's open fire.

"Sorry about the stench, old boy. Bloody awful out there, you know. Since *Spanish Tragedy* I've had nothing; nothing!" He rolled his eyes to heaven and raised his hands in wide supplication. "For god's sake, man, give me tobacco! Give me alcohol!"

Tuck assumed, rightly, that the man was referring to him. He quickly scanned the desk—there it was, in a little pouch the same size as the one he'd carried when—. *Well, seems I started this habit early anyway.* He grabbed the pouch and took out what must have been the tobacco—but where were the papers? He pawed the desk, looking for them."

"What *are* you doing, old son?"

"Looking for the rolling papers." Tuck continued his search, looking under papers, in drawers.

"What are you on about? The only thing we've got—*if* we've got any *papers*—are those stinking broadsheets with the bad reviews of *Spanish Tragedy*'s latest outing!" The Drama Queen was looking at Tuck strangely. "Use the bloody *pipe*! It's *there*, right in *front* of you!"

"Don't know what I was thinking," said Tuck. *Yes, I bloody well did! Hell, how do I know when cigarettes were invented? Apparently not yet.*

"Do we *have* any *alco*hol left"

They both surveyed the flat, taking in the numerous bottles (patently empty, as none of them were upright), and quickly decided they were out of booze. Tuck stopped himself before saying something monumentally stupid, like *I'll check the fridge for some.*

"This place *bores* me, Marlowe," drawled the Drama Queen. "It just re*minds* me of our *state* of desperate *pov*erty. So un*seem*ly for the great Marlowe and Kyd." (*He should take a peek in a mirror; he's young, but he's no kid.*) The Kid took a meditative puff on the pipe, folding his right arm across his narrow chest. The blue smoke curled languidly up to the coved ceiling, twelve feet above their heads. "Did they not *pay* you for your latest *voyage* to *la belle France*, my dearest Marlowe?"

Not knowing if he was paid, and if so, what he would have been paid for, Tuck just shook his head and shrugged his shoulders, in what he hoped was a passable imitation of the French stereotype.

It must have worked, for The Kid remarked, "*Demm* them all, anyway. Artists are treated a*bom*inably, but I do believe *spies* have it worse!" He chuckled, as he saw Tuck's eyes widen and his jaw drop open. "*Don't* be coy with *me*, Marlowe." The Kid's voice dropped to a conspiratorial whisper, and he leaned forward, toward Tuck. "You *talk* rather a lot when you're *drunk*, old man, and even more when you're a*sleep*." He sat back slightly, keeping his voice low. "You're *lucky* it's your old pal *Kyd* who hears you. I'm *watch*ing your *back*, you know…" he paused ominously, "and it *would*n't be *good*.…ah…*bus*iness for you to hold *out* on me, Marlowe. I could get you into *heaps* of trouble with the *Old Bill*." The Kid sat back fully now, drawing on the pipe, and looking self-satisfied.

Tuck, rather than be cowed by The Kid's remarks, laughed. He *guffawed.* He slapped his knees and, tears running from his eyes, shouted, "Bravo! Bravo!" and clapped his hands as if he were at the theater. "You simply *must* play the part of Mephistopheles for my new play, Kid." He wiped his streaming eyes. 'You simply *must*!"

Nonplussed, Kyd could only nod at first; then he tentatively began to chuckle; finally, seeing no guile in Tuck's eyes, he laughed loudly. "I should have *known* you planted those papers so I'd *find* them!" He was laughing merrily, not realizing that Tuck's laughter had stopped. "I can't *help* myself, and you *know* that." He giggled. "*Imagine!* I was ready to *sell you out!*"

How Tuck knew there would be a knife in his belt, he didn't know. Instinctively, his left hand went to his right hip, and his fingers clamped upon the dagger there. He drew it out, leapt from the chair, and lunged toward The Kid. He grabbed a hunk of The Kid's flowing brown locks, and yanked his head back, exposing the thin neck, to which he touched, gently but firmly, the tip of the knife.

"I shall slit you from here," Tuck touched the knife on the right side of Kid's neck, drawing it ever so slightly across to the left, under the earlobe, yet leaving a thin trail of blood, "to here," then deftly flicking the dagger upward, neatly slitting the lobe in half, and ignoring the Kid's choked cry, "if you ever, ever, *ever* go through my papers again." He released the hank of hair and put his knife back in its sheath. "Is that understood, my *dear* Kid?" Dumbly, touching the wound with his fingers and then looking at the blood on them, the ashen-faced Kyd nodded.

"That's settled then! Come, dear Kid; we shall venture to yon pub and see if anyone will buy us a drink! What say you?"

As if nothing had happened, Tuck held out Kyd's greatcoat for him, helping the shocked man put his arms in its frayed sleeves, and then adjusting the white scarf carefully around the wound he'd inflicted. "There. Good as new, old man." As for himself, he went, without a jacket, into the chilly London night.

Tuck had been right: they had showed up at the pub and were treated to drinks all night, thanks to Marlowe's *Tamburlaine*, still a huge hit on London stages. The two staggered home, best of friends, stumbling up the four long flights of stairs to their shared flat. Drunk and exhausted, they flopped onto their respective beds, not bothering to take off their clothes or shoes.

†

That night, Tuck had a dream. It started out much like his *Tamburlaine the Great* story, with a goat-herder becoming a hero, rising through the ranks to command a great army, only Tuck was the hero, with this beautiful woman by his side, and one son. In the dream, she did not stay in the tent while battles raged; she stayed by his side always. Her name, of course, was Zia.

Gradually the scenery changed, from the rolling desert sands and great dunes of the Middle East, to a green plain—miles and miles of green plain—undulating into the horizon toward a great mountain that towered in the east. He was at the head of a great, unending column of men, marching two by two, silently marching; the only sound he could hear was the jingling of goats' small silver bells as they trotted along beside the column of soldiers.

The soldiers were not British. They were dark, as Tamburlaine would have been dark, and they wore loincloths made of goat skin. Their chests were bare and bronzed, and their hair—each of them—was long and flowing, streaming out behind them, though there was no wind. They wore jewelry of finely worked silver and turquoise, and an orange gemstone he did not recognize.

In front of him was the palanquin holding his wife and small son. It was draped with white silk on four sides, to protect them from the sun, and it was carried by four of his finest young soldiers.

Although he carried a sword at his side, attached by a belt around his slim waist, the other soldiers had no weapons; they also had no provisions with them that Tuck could see. Everyone had a small leather pouch belted to his waist, but that was all. Yet no one tired; no one thirsted; no one hungered. They only marched, marched, marched; and the goats' bells tinkled softly in time with their steps.

In the distance, a rise appeared in front of them, sloping upward to a flattened top, a mesa. It sat there like a moon to the great sun of the mountain behind it and to the left. Tuck knew, in the dream, that this was where they were heading—to that great rise in the middle of the gentle green valleys through which they had been traveling for so long.

The rise was steeper and higher than it had appeared from the plain. At first, the ascent was gentle, but it grew increasingly more difficult to climb, and the verdant green gave way to gray rocks and sharp stones, interspersed with a sort of shrub with tendrils that curled around their ankles and slowed them down. *What fine rope that would make*, thought Tuck in his dream state. Up and up they climbed. Tuck could see the sweat streaming from the backs of the young men carrying the palanquin. Still, they did not complain, nor did they make any sound at all but an occasional grunt when a shrub caught their heel and made them stumble slightly.

They reached the top of the rise, and Tuck saw a great stone altar, carved out of the very rock, maybe fifty feet in front of him. The young men brought the palanquin to rest at the foot of the altar, before a trough of stone forming a semi-circle in front of it.

Now that they stood atop the plateau, Tuck felt a cool, fresh breeze blowing from his left, and heard clearly the sound of rushing water; he searched for its source. Walking to his left, leaving his troops standing there, he came to the edge of the mesa and saw a great river rushing past. He followed its path with his eyes, up, up, up the mountain that now towered so close to them, tumbling through a wide forest at the mountain's base. He thought he could see the source of the river, glinting—a small speck of silver—where the snow stopped and the junipers clung to the stony mountainside.

Turning, he saw the line of soldiers, stretching in a line for as far as he could see, all the way to the far horizon. He walked back to the palanquin and stood behind it slightly. He motioned for two of the young men to open the silk curtains and let his wife and son out into the fresh, cool breeze of the mesa.

This they did. Zia, stepping out, glanced his way and smiled at him—a radiant smile that warmed his heart—and Tuck smiled in his sleep, in his bed in the cold flat above the mean London streets. Then his son, only about four years old, stepped out, too, and smiled at him in the same loving way. Both mother and child then walked toward the altar.

Zia, with the help of two of the men, climbed onto the altar and laid down, her feet toward him, legs slightly spread, arms outstretched. He walked up to the altar, and stared at her; her eyes were closed against the sun, and she resembled a human crucifix. He looked to his right, and his son was no longer smiling. He was screaming, "Mama! Mama!" and stretching out his little hand to her. Tuck looked at Zia. Tears were streaming down her face; she was no longer smiling. Not a word did she utter; her eyes flew open and she fixed them upon him, pleading, pleading with her eyes not to do this horrible thing.

Tuck arms were raised high, and he looked up to see why. The sun was directly overhead, and he felt its heat shimmer through the breeze that still blowing coolly. Although he was blinded momentarily by the sun, he thought he saw the blade of a sword flashing, but he did not get the chance to make sure.

To his horror, he brought the sword down, with all his might, on his beloved wife, cleaving her in two with one fell swoop of his deadly sword. Appalled, he reached for her, letting his weapon of death fall, the sword clinking loudly on the stone of the altar. Her blood poured from the gaping wound, flowing off the altar and collecting in the trough below Tuck's feet.

He clutched at her chest, drawing out in his hand her still-beating heart. He held it up to the blazing sun, screaming, crying, in a language unintelligible to the myriad troops behind him.

"Zia! Zia! What have I done? *What have I done?*"

†

Tuck sat up in bed, shivering, crying, sweating. The Kid was next to him, shaking him, his face next to his, "Marlowe, old man! Wake *up*! Wake *up*!" The Kid was visibly frightened, his white face glowing eerily in the semi-dark of the room. "I *say*! What's the *mat*ter with you, old son?" He tried to laugh, but it came out as a choked gurgle, "Why, you sound as if you'd conjured the *dev*il him*self*!"

Tuck, recovering slightly, muttered, "Yes, I think I did, old friend. I think I did." He climbed out of bed and shuffled over to the desk. He lit the candle stub standing beside his manuscript, and then he sat down. "I'm afraid, Kid, that I need to write, right now. Try to get back to sleep. Sorry for waking you up." He turned back to the desk, took the quill out of its holder, filled it with ink, and continued writing *Doctor Faustus*.

12

Sponge

There's one thing I won't do. I won't sponge. I've never sponged.
Graham Green, *England Made Me*

Tuck drummed softly on the *tabla* between his knees. He was sitting on a cushion on a swept dirt floor, inside a sort of large, gazebo-like structure. There were approximately twenty men sitting in a circle with him, each with an instrument. The men were swarthy, sporting large mustaches, and speaking a different language. *It sounds like Greek. Remember when the wife and I went to the Greek Islands a few years ago?* He frowned slightly. *Was it a few years ago? Has it even happened yet?* Sighing, he tapped the drum, a little more loudly now. He felt, more than heard, the vibrations coming up through his fingers and resonating within his body.

In a few moments, a man rushed through the door, motioning them to start playing together. He was also gesturing toward the garden beyond, pointing to the people milling around what looked like an altar made of flowers. A fat man with a concertina nodded at those in the circle, counting out, Tuck supposed, a *one–two–three–four* for them to begin playing. Sure enough, music emanated from the group, a sort of joyful, yet sedate, tune. Tuck just followed along as best he could.

Then he could see, from where he was sitting, a woman in white enter from the right in front of the gazebo, while a young man, also in white, entered from the left. The crowd of people parted to let them walk up to the altar, where a man who might have been a priest (but not dressed like the ones Tuck had seen—or been—in his lifetime) facing the couple as they approached.

Concertina Man gave the nod to stop playing, but Tuck didn't see him, so intent was he on the scene in front of him. Tuck heard his drum's *ta-*Da, *ta-*Da echo dully in the silence and he sheepishly looked at the others, especially Concertina Man (who was livid), as if to say *Sorry*.

Still, Tuck couldn't keep his eyes off the couple being wed. She had some cornflower-blue, small flowers, and some lilies-of-the-valley woven into her long, thick, black hair, hair that hung to her slim waist. Her hips flared sensually from below the tiny waist, and she wiggled her bottom just a little as she stood waiting for the priest to finish. As she turned to kiss her husband, Tuck saw her beautiful profile, her cheek dimpling in his direction. So enthralled was he by the sight of her that he missed Concertina Man's cue to start, and he jumped when the band started playing the recessional music. Concertina Man gave Tuck another glare, and muttered something—no doubt about what he would do to Tuck when the music playing was all over.

That wasn't to be for a while, though. Song after song they played, the wedding guests and bride and groom now whirling madly, now slowly dancing, their bodies touching. Food was piled high on several tables around the garden, and when the band had a break, Tuck stuffed his face with food. There were olive and feta dishes, baklava, grape leaves stuffed with seasoned rice—all sorts of delights that not only tasted wonderful, but assured Tuck that he was, indeed, on a Greek island. Wine flowed, and even Concertina Man mellowed, no longer acting like he wanted to murder Tuck for nearly ruining the wedding ceremony.

For some reason, no one expected Tuck to talk, which was fine with him. People talked very loudly to him, when anyone bothered to speak to him, that is, as if he were deaf. *Maybe they think I'm deaf.* He pondered that thought briefly. *Works for me.*

The celebration lasted long into the night, the revelers heading home when the sky was tinged pink to begin a new day. Tuck had no idea where he was supposed to go, and drunk and tired, he just leaned against one of the pillars of the gazebo and passed out, his clothes dampened by the early morning's dew.

He was shaken awake by Concertina Man after what seemed like only a few minutes; the sun, however, was high in the sky, so it might have been about noon. Concertina motioned for him to get up! get up! and follow him, so Tuck did, his head aching and his tongue feeling fuzzy. Concertina led him to a *taverna* on the seashore, where Tuck was given large amounts of dark, steaming coffee, and a nice fresh pita slathered with olive oil for his breakfast. Tuck smiled his thanks, but Concertina seemed agitated. He kept tapping his foot, watching Tuck eat, and looking out at the harbor, in particular, toward a large schooner with a Greek flag flying from its mast; a British flag flew just below it.

Tuck took his time eating, as he wasn't sure what he was going to be required to do next. When he couldn't stretch it out any longer, Concertina nearly dragged him from the *taverna* and led him to the ship at which he'd been staring. They went up the gangplank, and to Tuck's joy, he saw all the musicians from the wedding, along with the groom and some of the other male guests. They were all stripped to the waist and barefoot, and all had a peculiarly shaped knife strapped to the sides of their white, wide breeches. Tuck waved at everyone, but they just looked very annoyed. Concertina was gesticulating wildly, pointing at Tuck and in the general direction of the gazebo, and everyone's head nodded, up-and-down, up-and-down, as if to say, *Of course, we wouldn't expect anything else from this idiot.*

The captain, too—Tuck assumed he was the captain; he was white, not dark like the rest of them, and he sported a sea captain's hat—first seemed to reprimand Concertina and then agree with him. Tuck got the distinct impression that they had all waited for him, and they weren't happy that he'd been late getting to the boat. *They must need me for something, though, or they wouldn't have waited.*

The ship prepared to set sail and Tuck helped. The captain sent him to undo the ropes that tied them to the dock. Along the shore beside the quay stood all the womenfolk, waving to their loved ones. Tuck could see the bride of the day before, her hand waving slowly, then touching her lips and blowing a kiss to her beloved. Tuck pretended she was waving to him, and he blew her a kiss back. Someone shoved him roughly from behind, pushing him so hard he fell to the deck; it was the groom. Sheepishly, Tuck got to his feet, bowing his head as if to say, *Sorry.* Somehow, Tuck instinctively knew there was no one on that shore that *was* waving to him; he was alone in this world.

Within a few minutes, the ship was ready to set sail. It glided out of the harbor on the turquoise water, while the crew lined the ship's rail, saying goodbye to their loved ones. Tuck stood and waved too; this time, no one stopped him.

Only an hour or so out from the tiny island which sat like an orange jewel in the sea, Tuck realized why they had waited for him. The ship dropped anchor, and all the men who had knives now took off their billowy trousers. Tuck watched, fascinated, as a thick rope was tied to the waist of one of the men. This man clambered to the ship's rail, poised himself, balancing like an acrobat, clenching the sharp knife between his teeth, and then he dove cleanly into the water. The rope played out after him. Down, down the man stayed. *How can he hold his breath that long?* Tuck was amazed. *It must be four minutes now.* Finally, the man broke the surface of the water, grinning broadly and holding up a huge sponge, dripping with seawater. Everyone cheered, including Tuck, as the man, with some help, climbed up and threw the now-dead sponge into the hold of the ship.

Then, in unison, the crew turned to look at Tuck.

Uh-oh. My turn.

13

Butter

History is a nightmare from which I'm trying to awake.
James Joyce, *Ulysses*

Tuck awoke, startled from a deep sleep. Someone was screaming as if she were being killed; that sound was followed quickly by the sound of a rooster crowing; it sounded as if both screamer and rooster were beside him.

"OW-W-W-W! FUCK!" Sitting up to get his bearings in the darkness, Tuck whacked his head on an overhead beam, which sent him straight back down on the bed. Putting his hand up to his head, he felt blood oozing from the spot he'd hit. "Where am I, an attic?" He heard giggling nearby. "What? What? Who's here?" Tuck's voice sounded high and...and...*female. It had to happen sooner or later.* Tuck sighed deeply, and he raised his head very, very slowly this time. "Who's there? I've cracked my head open." Pushing himself by his hands, he could feel he was lying on something distinctly organic. *Hay. It smells like hay.*

A girl's voice answered from, not from next to him, but not from too far away, either. "You're daft altogether, so you are, Siobhán." The disembodied voice giggled again. "Were ye dreamin' of that fine stable boy,

Tony, again? Bejaysus, he's a bit of alright; dreamt of him now 'n' then meself."
He could hear the sound of a match being struck, and in a moment he could
put a face to the voice he'd heard. "Now, let's take a look atcha."

"What's your name?" Tuck asked slowly, fascinated with the sound of
his own voice.

"What's me name! Jesus, Mary, Joseph, and holy Saint Patrick, that
crack on the head's done you damage!" She skootched over from her straw
mattress to Tuck's, holding up a lantern and being careful not to bruise her own
head, which was cap-covered, with dozens of brown curls tumbling every which
way, full of bits of straw. She leaned over and Tuck could see the outline of her
perky breasts under the thin white nightdress. "Well, would you look at that,"
she said, pushing aside Tuck's own white cap, now stained with blood. "You've
gone and done it now, Siobhán." Tuck winced as she pushed and prodded at
the egg-shaped bump now rising through his auburn ringlets. "Owwww! Stop
that!"

"Sorry, it's got to be done. That's a nasty bump you've got there, missy,
and that's not a word of a lie I'm tellin'." She thought for a moment, then said,
"Do ye think ye'd be up ta doin' the milkin'? I hate to wake Cook at this hour to
have her dress that wound."

"Milkin'?" Tuck hoped his look was appropriately shocked enough that
whoever-she-was would decide there'd be no milking of cows for "Siobhán"
today.

"Yes, ya daft git—that's what we do first thing in the mornin', as you
well know. Then it's the eggs we'll be gatherin' and the pigs we'll be sloppin',
and… sure what am I tellin' you this for, you know it like you know your own
name." At Tuck's befuddled look, she recanted. "Then again, you don't look
like ya *do* know yer own name, and that's a fact." She rolled to her side of the
straw and started taking off her nightclothes. "Ye can be comin' with me, at any
rate, even if yer good for *no* thing this mornin'." She turned back to look at him,
and her breasts, with their perfect pink nipples, were one of the prettiest sights
he thought he'd ever seen. "Have ye no shame? What are ye starin' at, ya daft

gell? Haven't ye seen these little babas, day in and day out, for the past two years?" She huffed a bit and turned back to her dressing. "Get yer clothes on. We're late enough as it is." She continued muttering under her breath, while Tuck—carefully avoiding the roof beam—decided to try and find his clothes.

While smoothing on the rough cotton underwear he'd found in a heap of clothes beside the straw bed, he couldn't help but notice and appreciate his own lovely body, running both his hands lightly over his breasts and then down his slim waist, hips, and thighs.

"Would ye ever stop admirin' yersel' and get ready, for the love of God?" Tuck's barn mate tsked in the corner. "Lord a'mighty, ye'll need to confess yer unnatural love for yerself to Father Murphy come Sunday." *Sotto voce* she said, "First she's lookin' at me, then she can't keep her hands off herself. I never—"

"I'm ready!" Tuck exclaimed, hoping the other girl would let her own name slip somehow so he could call her by it. The two girls headed over to a ladder, which they rapidly descended, and which landed them in the main part of the barn.

It was much larger than Tuck had thought when he only had their small loft to judge the place by. This barn was sizeable. Hanging from every wall were farm implements, old-fashioned in looks, but shiny—not rusted at all. All along one wall were the cows' stalls, and in each one a fine Guernsey or Holstein waited—some patiently, some impatiently, if the hoof-stamping and half-moos were anything to go by. There was a large viaduct, made of the same stone as the floors, down the middle of the barn's floor, presumably for the farm hand (*Oh, wait—that's probably me*) to sweep the cow dung into and then flush out. At the moment, this viaduct was clean.

A friendly border collie yipped his way through the crack in the barn door. He greeted each girl, sniffing the young hands appreciatively and then giving them a lick for luck. Although the morning's chill was in the air, there was a warmth in the place that seeped into Tuck. *This isn't the worst place I've been, that's for sure.*

"Are ye able for this Siobhán? Yer forty shades of green." Not-Siobhán made up her mind. "Yer not to be near those cows this mornin', missy. The state yer in, yer likely to be kicked by every cow in the place. They know when their milker's away with the fairies." She pointed to a stack of hay near the back, under their loft. "Sit there while I do the job for both of us, and do sing us the little song the cows like. They allus give better milk when ye sing. 'Tis only curdles we get when I be doin' the singin'." Not-Siobhán went to the far stall, pulling her milking stool and pail from a nook in the wall, nearly opposite from where Tuck sat nonplussed.

Not-Siobhán went in to the first cow, and it wasn't long before Tuck heard the steady *tsss-tsss* of the milk hitting the pail. Part of a white cap peeped out from behind the cow's rump. "Where's that music, Siobhán? Don't tell me you've forgot that 'n' all—you who's been singin' since you was born!" The hat disappeared, and there was some more *tsss*-ing before Tuck saw the white cap reappear. Even the cap looked miffed, from his viewpoint; it went with its wearer's exasperated sigh. "Don't be shy now. These cows need ye. We all love to hear ye do a party piece."

The milking stopped for a moment as Not-Siobhán reminisced. "Do ye remember that Christmas, right here at the Maguires, when we were first taken on and we the both of us were so terrified of bein' away from home? They had that table set so lovely, with the Christmas crackers and all, even for the two of us, and they wanted us to sing a song together, seein' as we're sisters." She chuckled, although her voice was so muffled by having her forehead against the cow, she could have been coughing, Tuck wasn't sure. "You piped up, 'Eimear's favorite is "Black Velvet Band," can we sing that?'" She was laughing hard now; Tuck heard the sound of the stool slipping and her falling into the hay, against the wall of the stall. "Oh, 'twas a tonic to see their faces when you asked could we sing my favorite song—"Black Velvet Band"—on CHRISTMAS, of all days!"

Tuck didn't hear the sound of his sister getting back on her stool and continue the milking, he was so delighted to finally know her name. "Ah, Eimear, that was a laugh alright. 'Black Velvet Band' indeed!" His laughter was more from relief than humor; "Black Velvet Band" could be the national anthem, for all he knew. "Well, I won't be singin' that to the cows, anyway!" Tuck said merrily.

The white cap peeked out yet again. "What d'ye mean? It's the cows' favorite." The frill on the cap moved back and forth. "I'd say they can sing it themselves." She got up and moved into the next stall, plopping herself onto the three-legged stool, and slapping the cow's flank as she did so. "C'mon, Clara, let's be havin' ya. Miss Siobhán's done cracked her head so hard she's forgot the tune. Let's help her out." Eimear's voice—nearly as awful as she'd made it out to be, but not quite—sang out,

Her eyes, they shine like the diamonds;

You'd swear she was queen of the land.

And her hair hung over her shoulders,

Tied up with a black velvet band!

"Does that stir anything to life in yer brain, Siobhán? No?" The white cap bobbed out of sight. "How 'bout you, Clara?" As if in answer, the cow mooed mightily and kicked the pail of milk over. Both girls laughed hysterically, wiping their eyes with the hem of their aprons.

"Well, that's taught me!" said Eimear, as she picked up her now-empty pail and her stool, and moved to the next cow. "Oh, Missus Maguire's not going to be happy with that spilled milk. Siobhán, make yerself useful and go see if the cat's about. Old Puss'd love to have that creamy milk for herself, even mixed with straw, so she would." Eimear went into peals of laughter again, barely able to spit out, "And-she-won't-be-cryin'-over-it-neither!" Happier than he'd been in a long time, Tuck ventured through the opening in the barn door, ostensibly to search for the cat, but mainly so he could see where he was.

From the comparative warmth of the barn, the early morning chill of the still morning came as quite a shock. To the right of him, the sun was just beginning to rise, the horizon a dark-pinkish glow, run through with bright orange, letting him know which way was east. Directly ahead of him was a low outbuilding, from whence emanated the snorting and hoof-stamping of maybe half a dozen horses. Off to the left stood a large, white, two-storied house, looming in the dimness like a huge, crouching animal. No light showed through the mullioned windows, and only a thin plume of smoke came from the chimneys at each gabled end. There were few trees around the home, although Tuck could make out a small woods further north of it. The house and its outbuildings, including the outhouse (placed a respectful distance from the house-dwellers, but in close proximity to the barn), stood on a gentle rise. Tuck scanned the horizon, turning slowly in a circle, but saw no other houses or barns. They were miles from anything. *How peaceful it is*, thought Tuck.

He felt something brush his ankle. Startled, he realized it was just the cat—a big, gray mouser who matched the dim surroundings. Tuck tried to pick her up, but the cat scratched and clawed, meowing loudly.

"Well, be that way, then! See if I show you where the cream is, you naughty kitty." Tuck surprised himself at the lilt in his voice. *Bejaysus!* He giggled. *I've got a brogue and all!* The cat padded a few steps away, toward the barn, then stopped, looking over its left shoulder with a look that said, *"Do you reckon I have had a bump on the head, too? What do you think I came over here for—to see you? I think not."* She swished her tail and haughtily padded—not ran—to the barn door.

Tuck tried out a few bars of the song he'd heard Eimear sing. "Her eyes, they shine like the diamonds. . ." *Not bad! Not bad at all. My voice is definitely better as a girl than as a guy.*

The milking done, Eimear led Tuck over to the big white house, where she knocked loudly on the back door before walking in. "Don't want to surprise Cook; need to give her time to hide the whiskey bottle," she said in a low voice, winking slyly. Tuck giggled. They walked into a big kitchen, wiping their shoes carefully on the woven mat by the door, and tiptoeing in. Cook, Tuck surmised, was the tall, thin stick standing at the woodburning stove and stirring a huge pot of something.

"Is that porridge ready yet, Cook?" Eimear loudly whispered. Cook just shook her head *no* and pointed peremptorily at two of the eight chairs around the wood-planked table. Giving Tuck a laughing look and crooking her finger for Tuck to follow, Eimear tiptoed exaggeratedly over to the table.

"We'll have none of your antics this mornin', missy," barked Cook in a low voice. "You're ever so late from the milking, and you don't seem to have brought me any fresh eggs."

"Oh, dreadful sorry, Cook—but didn't I break every last one of them on the way over here. There was a large goat, y'see, and he charged me like, and…" Cook, at first ready to reprimand Eimear, realized she was being teased, and gave a good-natured, toothy grin. "All right, missy—where are they then?" Tuck could tell this was a game often played between the two of them. Eimear produced two from under her cap, three from her pinnie pockets, and two more from Tuck's pockets. "Oh, they're lovely and brown, aren't they, girls?" Cook placed them carefully on the cutting board beside the big Belfast sink. "They'll go grand with the rashers and puddin' for the Master and Missus this mornin'." Cook's pointy-featured face broke into little smiley pieces. "You're both very good, really. How I wish your mum and dad could see how you've turned out." She turned quickly away from them, but not before Tuck saw the tears glisten in both of her eyes. Tuck glanced over at Eimear, but she, too, was silent for once; silent and thoughtful.

"Well," said Eimear quickly, "I wonder would they be so happy if they could see what Siobhán's gone and done to herself this very mornin'. Would you ever look at this bump, Cook?"

Cook whirled around, rushing over to Tuck so quickly he didn't have time to think. Eimear came over, too, and all Tuck could see were their bosoms, rising and falling, rising and falling, in front of him as their eyes searched and their fingers probed and prodded the bruise on his head.

"Oh bejaysus that's a—"

"Would ya believe she forgot herself and hit the beam when—"

"—what a goose egg that is!"

"—she woke."

"We'd better get that cleaned—

"She forgot the cows' song 'n' all—"

"—before it gets infected. Hand me a bit of the—"

"—didn't remember the Christmas neither."

"—lye over by the Aga and—"

"Will she be all right, Cook?" Eimear's voice was soft and worried.

Instead of heaving bosoms, Tuck saw two pairs of eyes looking into his, concerned. He opened his eyes wide and tried to look straight ahead.

"Yes," they both said. Then Cook and Eimear looked at each other. "Yes." And they both sighed with relief. "We won't have to tell the Missus, neither," said Cook. For some reason, that seemed to be a good thing. Tuck wondered why.

†

After a bracing breakfast of the best oatmeal he'd ever tasted, homemade bread slathered with pure white butter, and a big mug of strong tea, the girls left Cook to make breakfast for the rest of the household. The sun had risen; it would be a clear, cold day—not cold enough to be icy, but cold enough where the warmth of the barn was preferable to being outside. As Tuck had suspected, it was his and Eimear's job to muck out the cow stalls. It was also their job to muck out the horse stalls, slop the pigs (who had their own spot in a sty beyond the horse stalls; Tuck couldn't see it from the barn that morning), feed the chickens, and do every dirty job around the farm there was to do.

At lunchtime, Cook rang a large triangle that hung outside the back door, and Tuck met the three field hands who'd come back for their meal. They were a good-natured lot, Irish too, and there was much laughing and craíc as Eimear regaled them with, among other stories, the tale of Siobhán's head injury and resultant amnesia. Adjudging Siobhán to have truly lost her memory, Eimear and the farm hands, with a little help from Cook, started from the beginning and told Tuck his life story—as only the Irish can. From the stories he heard over the next few days, along with the things Cook had mentioned that morning, Tuck began to figure out why he was here, a thirteen-year-old milkmaid, in Ireland, in 1913.

✝

Eimear and Siobhán were the only two surviving children out of six born to the luckless couple Declan and Bridget Maguire, originally from County Leitrim. Declan, the third of eight brothers, not only knew the farm would never be his, but from somewhere—nobody knew from where—he had acquired a taste for the finer things in life, stubbornly believing he, unlike anyone in the family in all the preceding centuries, would get them.

Declan had the mistaken idea that if he were a solider in the British Army, he would reach his lofty goals. He liked the British uniforms—he had seen the soldiers who strutted around Enniskillen carrying their guns—and firmly believed the Brits would end up in charge of Ireland. He wanted to "work for the winnin' side," he would say, none too wisely. For if there was anything the Maguires hated more than their hurley team losing to Mayo, it was the Brits, plain and simple. Declan would have been booted out of Manorhamilton if he hadn't left of his own accord, on a gray, wet day in June, 1887, with his young bride Bridget tearfully in tow. Her family, the Dolans, was appalled that she had deserted her family in favor of the good-for-nothing-but-cannon-fodder Declan Maguire, and no one offered them a lift to Enniskillen, or saw the dismal, deluded couple off.

After walking several miles on the winding, pot-holed, muddy road, they entered County Fermanagh, where fewer people—eventually—recognized the traitors. On the south side of the Leitrim border, the normally warm-hearted occupants of the few carts that passed Declan and Bridget would not give the bedraggled couple a lift, the drivers keeping their eyes fixed on the road ahead as soon as they recognized, from behind, the short, thin man and his plump little wife, holding hands and each carrying a small, tattered case bound with rope. Now that the couple was on the busier main road, it wasn't long before a very nice coach indeed came by, the four proud horses halting in unison beside them. An arm with a white-gloved hand emerged from the window, imperiously waving them to join the occupant of the carriage.

The mud-spattered couple, grateful for a lift at last, opened the carriage door and tried to climb in with their cases. "Please do leave those dreadful bags on the road. The driver will get them for you," a brandy-soaked, cultured voice implored. Declan and Bridget dropped their damp cardboard suitcases on the road as directed. Sure enough, the driver hopped down to retrieve them, treating the boxes as if they were made of fine leather. The young couple looked up as they heard their meager belongings being strapped to the roof of the coach; their hands—her right, his left—were tightly held together. They looked at each other and smiled, elated, then, tearing their eyes away from each other's face, they looked at their benefactor.

Although the portly gentleman sitting across from them did not smell like he had been drinking, they knew it had not been very long since he had. He had what the Maguires liked to call a "brandy head," the florid features of a frequent tippler of that particular spirit. His eyes struggled to emerge from the many layers of fat surrounding them; his nose was bulbous in the extreme, with an extra lump or two on its end for good measure; the cheeks were pockmarked and pitted. A cravat, of a type not often seen at this hour of the morning by the rich (and never by the poor), bravely encircled the neck, the circumference of which was the same as the man's head. Although the man's clothing was made of the finest material the young couple had ever seen, they couldn't help but notice the large greasy stain—butter? gravy?—which started on his whitest-of-white shirts and encroached on the brocaded waistcoat, the buttons of which were in danger of bursting and causing one of the newlyweds eye damage. Instinctively, the couple inched closer together for safety, raising their four hands together to their two chins.

"You look alarmed, children. There is no need to look alarmed," the man sputtered regally. "You are quite safe with me." He then attempted what for him must have been a smile. He was not successful, probably due to lack of practice, the small yellow teeth flashing momentarily in the sea of flab surrounding them. The young people smiled weakly back at them. (They may not have had all the teeth God had intended, but the ones they had were far whiter, they were sure.)

"May I ask, children, why you travel this poor excuse of a road on this miserable, wet day? What are your names, and where are you going?" The fat man made no attempt to smile this time, nor did he introduce himself; his words may have sounded like a question, but they were said by a man who was used to getting answers—straight answers—from the menials who did his bidding.

Declan cleared his throat before speaking, for he sensed the import of what he was about to say; when he did speak, Brandy Head visibly cringed at the young man's poor grammar and thick, countrified speech habits. Mercifully, Declan and Bridget were staring into each other's eyes for the thousandth time that morning, and missed the fat man's wince. It might have kept Declan from saying his piece, the consequences of which were to alter the course of their young lives forever.

"Eh-*hem*. Eh—*hem*. *Hem*." There was more phlegm than usual in Declan's throat. Tankin' yew, Sore. Tankin' yew; *hem*. Me woife 'n' eye be headin' fer Enniskillen *tow*-win, Sore. We was tinkin', er, well, I was tinkin', and me woife, Bridget here" (at the mention of her name, he just had to look into her green, adoring eyes; they gave him courage), "she a-grrreeees, Sore, that I should jyne the Brits...dat is, the *British* Air-mee." Here Declan hoped he gave the word "British" all the pomp it required, and he sat up straighter, as if he were already attired in His Majesty's fine brown uniform. Bridget tightened her grip on his left hand, squeezing it until his fingertips went white.

"You desire to join the British Army? When you are so clearly . . . shall we say . . . *not British* in the usual sense of the word?"

Bridget's auburn curls bobbed up and down, and Declan's pudding-bowl-cut brown hair swayed as the couple nodded vigorously, as if enthusiastic nodding alone could make their dream a reality. The coach happened, at the moment, to hit a particularly big pothole, which emphasized the couple's nods and nearly landed them in the lap of Brandy Head.

"May I ask *why*?" Brandy Head placed his walking stick between his thick knees, his white-gloved hands atop its gold head.

Declan glanced at his beloved as if to say, *In for a penny; in for a pound!* "It's down to the uni-farms, Sore, dat's what's caught me eyes like. I've nivver seed such fine uni-farms, Sore," then he hastily added, "'ceptin' a-coarse, yore's, Sore." Declan regarded the man with more interest than previously; "Doze air some mighty fine cloze yew've got dare, and not a word of a lie dare, Sore, or may the divvel take me, Sore. Very fine dey air, Sore." He remembered his manners. "Tankin' yew, Sore." He touched his forelock, as no cap was available to him. That was one thing he hoped would change in the near future.

"You're saying, if I understand you correctly, that you would risk your very life—and the heartbreak of your lovely wife (at this, dismayed but loving looks exchanged between Declan and Bridget)—to wear fine clothes?"

The heads had been bobbing assent until Brandy Head came to the last four words, when they slowed and then stopped, the young minds realizing for the first time the real basis for Declan's career decision. No one had every put it so succinctly to them before. However, it was a long-held dream for Declan, and he wasn't about to fall at the first hurdle. With one quick look at Bridget, and her answering squeeze to his numb fingers, he looked Brandy Head straight in the eyes and said, "Yes, Sore. Dat's right, Sore. For da uni-farm, yes."

Brandy Head's small smile was lost in fat, but a noise the newlyweds thought was a belch rumbled from somewhere below the fine waistcoat. He tapped his cane twice, in an effort to steady his voice, before saying, "I trust you know something of horses." Declan nodded. Sure hadn't he often had a flutter on the gee-gees, hoping to win a few bob? "What if I were to offer you, shall we say, a less life-threatening way of earning your living, one in which you would still wear fine clothes?"

"Oh, Sore! Dat would be grr-*ate* Sore!" The heads bobbed furiously and in unison. Any career that was not life-threatening, yet offered fine clothing, would be preferable—indeed it would. If the Maguires and the Dolans could see him now! Only a few hours out of the village, and here he was, nearly rich and famous already. "I'll take it, Sore!" He added quickly, touching his brown hair again, as did Bridget her auburn, "Tankin' yew kindly, Sore. Yew won't be sorry."

†

That was how Declan became Mr. Cudahy-Conyngham's carriage driver; old Gilligan, his current driver, suffered from lumbago and could no longer stay up all hours, waiting in the cold damp air, and sitting atop the carriage, for Cudahy-Conyngham to leave his club, or his card game, or his mistress, or the theater. Gilligan missed his warm bed and warmer wife, who had died waiting for him, it seems, three months ago.

Gilligan stayed until he had taught Declan all he knew. He found the young man to be a quick study and a dab hand with the horses. For his part, Declan surprised himself: he liked working, after all—and he looked terrific in the black uniform and smart cap; Bridget told him so. Although the pay wasn't great, the young couple was given a spacious apartment over the stables, and all the food and medical care they needed or wanted.

After the twins, Bridget had had a stillborn baby boy, then Eimear. The twins, Declan Jr. and Devin, died together; they had jumped from the roof of the stable. Eimear was only three, but she remembered standing in the forecourt of the stable yard and watching her five-year-old brothers climb the ladder left out by a stable hand. The twins were saying, "We can fly! We can fly!" as they toddled up the rungs, and "Watch, Eimear; watch us!" when they reached the roof. Watch she did, as the two boys held hands and leapt toward her, while she clapped her hands excitedly. She still remembered the red blood pouring from their little bodies, face down in the muck of the yard. Now her own screams in the night, the screams that could not wake her brothers, still woke anyone sleeping near her; it was what woke Tuck on his first morning at the farm.

Hearing her five-year-old screaming, Bridget had run out of the Big House, where she worked in the kitchen, leaving two-year-old Conor playing with his blocks by the Aga stove, and tiny, beautiful Siobhán, conceived on New Year's Eve, 1899, in celebration of the *fin de siècle*, asleep in her Moses basket in a corner by the kitchen window. Distracted with grief, Bridget tried to scoop up the twins' lifeless bodies into her ample lap as she knelt in the blood, cooing and singing softly in between the sobs that racked her body. Eimear just held mummy's head with her left arm and sucked the thumb of her right hand.

They must have been out there a long time, because Declan, who had driven Mr. Cudahy-Conyngham to the racetrack shortly before the incident, came out of the kitchen door, sobbing and carrying Conor, who was screaming and screaming. While Bridget had been out in the courtyard tending to her dead twins, Conor, bored with his blocks, had reached up to the big steaming pot of potatoes on the hob. The heavy pot tipped, first dumping its steaming contents all over him before landing on his body, writhing on the kitchen floor. Declan had come in by the front door, whistling and happy over the two hundred bob he'd won at the track that day, only to find his son in agony on the floor. The child died two days later from the burns.

All three children were buried, in the finest coffins two hundred bob could buy, over the border in Leitrim, where the Maguires and the Dolans welcomed their son and daughter back into the fold, the past forgiven in the aftermath of the tragedy; apparently, even Declan and Bridget had suffered enough. Mr. Cudahy-Conyngham was more than a little miffed to discover, the day after the tragedies, that Declan and Bridget had left their posts without a word of notice breathed to him or anyone else on his staff.

†

Declan and Bridget tried to fit back into life in Leitrim, but found they could not. On a cold, wet day in September, on their eighteenth wedding anniversary, they decided to end it all. They weighted their clothing—the finery they once wore in Enniskillen, not so well-fitting twelve years on—with stones from the shore of Lough Gill. They walked in together, hand in hand, giving each other a last loving look before they sank below the brown, choppy waves. They left no note, but someone on the far side of the Lough found Declan's fine, though waterlogged, cap; the finder dried it well and wore it often.

Eimear and Siobhán, a year later to the day of their parents' suicides, found their mother's once-white frilly cap caught on a branch from a fallen log, near the shore, and near the spot where the couple had walked in to their watery deaths. Eimear boiled the cap over and over, trying to restore its color, but all she managed to do was fade the embroidered initials, *BDM*. It was September 8, 1912: Siobhán's twelfth birthday.

†

Tuck knew, after hearing the tale, that Declan had been Zia. And Bridget had been him—Tuck. Bridget, with the auburn curls. Tuck fingered his own auburn ringlets thoughtfully, and looked over at Eimear, carefully rolling her wayward brown hair into a tight bun at the nape of her neck. *How is it possible, to be two people at the same time? How does this all work?* His eyes filled with tears. *How long will I be with Eimear?* Impulsively, Tuck reached over to her and hugged her with all his might. She started to protest, laughing, then hugged Tuck back fiercely, smoothing his auburn curls with one work-worn hand, and rocking him gently to and fro.

14

St. Moritz

Speak in French when you can't think of the English for a thing.
Lewis Carroll, *Through the Looking Glass*

"The next skier up," blared a voice through the loudspeaker, "is the famous Henri Oreiller, skiing for France!" Tuck couldn't hear the loudspeaker, but the spectators could. Tuck was waiting with other skiers at the top of what looked like a long run, a slalom course dotted with large moguls. Fully decked out in ski gear, he was sliding his skis back and forth on the packed snow as he prepared to enter the gate. *My god, look at these long skis. Classic. They must be from about the late '40s, maybe early '50s.* Through the vintage ski goggles, he could see people lined up on either side of the run, a crowd continuing, he supposed, past his line of vision. Quick glances to his left and right showed Olympic badges and signs, in French first, then English.

Holy shit! Is this the Olympics? He felt excited. *The Olympics! Me!* He glanced down at his skis. *If it's Alpine skiing, it must be 1936 or after. From the look of these skis, I'd say "after."* He tried to remember where previous Winter Olympics had been held, the ones whose skiers might have used these particular skis. If he could figure that out, he'd know which course he was about to ski. Rapidly calculating, he came up with a plausible answer. *I'll bet this is Moritz. I sure hope I'm one of the good skiers. French would be nice. Hell, I must be good or I wouldn't be here.*

He muttered under his breath, "Hi, how are you? I'm Tuck." Sure enough, it came out, "*Bonjour; comment ça va?" Je suis* Tuck." *Yes! I'm French. I'll bet I know this mountain pretty good.*

Someone was motioning to him, saying in American English, "C'mon, buddy, we haven't got all day." The man turned to his obviously American coworker. "These damn Frenchies. They think they can do whatever they want. Stuck-up assholes!"

Tuck smiled at them, though they couldn't see him through his ski mask, and sweetly told them, in French, "Fuck off. I'm going to win this race, and I'll see your sorry asses later." Tuck waved as he said this, and the Americans waved back, laughing at him and nudging each other.

Tuck positioned himself in the gate, testing his knees and other joints. *Like a well-oiled machine. Nice.* He saw the big Timex clock slightly to his right, ticking down the seconds. TEN. . . NINE. . . EIGHT. . . SEVEN. . . SIX. . . FIVE. . . FOUR. . . THREE. . . TWO. . .

Tuck was gone as the second hand clicked into place. For good or ill, he was off. The bystanders blurred, becoming part of the mountain, a multi-colored stripe, giving him an idea in which direction the slope was heading. The run was slick; he was not the first skier today. With incredible precision, he skirted every mogul and flag, weaving his way down as if he had been born for this moment. Tuck wondered how fast he was going; he didn't think he'd ever gone this fast before. His blood thrilled through him, every molecule of his being knowing that, in this round at least, he had done his absolute best.

There was the finish—he could see the red barrier looming beyond it, seeming to rush at him. Crossing the final marker, he turned sharply, stopping perfectly, inches from the barrier. He turned and waved at the crowd, both poles over his head, as he glided back toward them. Now he could hear the triumphant voice through the loudspeakers. "Henrie Oreiller! Il est la victoire avec un temps de. . ." The French supporters drowned out the rest of the announcer's speech. They swarmed past the orange-colored rope barriers, heading for Tuck. Someone had brought champagne—he heard the pop—and before he knew it, he was holding up a glass full of it, surrounded by his adoring countrymen and -women, and having his picture taken by scores of photographers. Flashbulbs popped and melted the snow upon which they fell.

What a moment! Could it get any better than this? This is what I've always dreamed of! Tuck felt tears prick the back of his eyelids. *Oh, no. No tears. I don't care how emotional the French might be—no tears!* He swallowed his joy and kept smiling broadly. He removed his skis and a waiting Olympic worker took them, promising, Tuck hoped—he wasn't completely sure of his French—to dry them and wax them in preparation for the next day. *The next day. Ah. This isn't over yet, is it?*

†

Back in his room at the Olympic Village, he took a long, steamy shower and then shaved, rubbing the steam from the mirror and noting his facial features: green, deep-set eyes that were almost Oriental looking and somewhat close together; a large, but handsome, nose; wavy brown hair; evenly spaced teeth in a mouth with full, straight lips. *I still look pretty damn good, actually, considering all I've been through. I thought I'd look different, somehow, from what I remember.* It had been a long time—lifetimes—since he'd seen himself in a mirror. He smiled at his reflection and noticed he had deep laugh lines etched into each of his tanned cheeks. *I hope I'm still popular with the ladies.* He strolled naked into the next room, the bedroom, his muscled, perfectly toned body moving easily on the carpeted floor. He changed into designer jeans he found hanging in his closet, and donned a sweater he found folded neatly in the blonde-wood bureau next to the matching full-sized bed. Someone must have entered his room while he was showering—a disconcerting thought—for a copy of that day's *Le Monde* was on the white eyelet duvet. The masthead told him it was January 30, 1948, the opening day of the Winter Olympics in Saint-Moritz.

There he was, in a large picture on the front page, smiling and waving. He was wearing his Olympic ski suit, and a close-fitting ski cap, so the picture must have been taken yesterday, or maybe this morning, early. He read that he was born on October 5, 1925, and that he was known as the "madman of downhill skiing." He smiled. *That's what they called me back home. "The madman."* He stopped, thoughtful. *Wherever home is. A long way from here.* He sighed a little, and kept reading. It was hard for him to translate all the French, but he gathered that he had dared the Olympic skiers from the other participating nations to try and beat him. *I'm a cocky little bastard, that's for sure.* It made him doubly glad that he had told the American guys, before he'd made his run today, to fuck off.

He also gleaned from the article the fact that today's run was only the first qualifier; he would be skiing again tomorrow, and the day after that. He had to keep winning; it wasn't over yet. *Somehow,* he thought to himself as he slipped on a maroon cashmere jacket over his dark blue turtleneck sweater, *I think I'm going to win this one.* "I'm going for gold," he said out loud. Then he laughed at himself, wondering where he had picked up this abundance of confidence. He folded the paper in half, and put it in his suitcase, standing open on a low pine table near the bureau. A knock—*shave-and-a-hair-cut*—came to his door; he opened it before the *"two-bits,"* like he used to do with his best buddy.

It *was* his best buddy—Greg. *Unbelievable.* "Who's gonna get lucky tonight?" Greg said. Tuck laughed, punching him on the shoulder.

"It's gonna have to be you, *mon ami*; I'm in the Olympics, remember?"

"Like you could *ever* let us forget!" The two men walked down the hall, speaking in French, and understanding each other's every word and nuance as if they were the American friends Tuck remembered from his past.

†

Tuck behaved himself that night at the celebratory dinner held in his honor. Although "Henrie" had oodles of confidence, the pragmatic French team and their coach were less assured that they would bring home the gold medal. The captain of the team had decided they would have a celebration dinner—*sans* hard liquor, of course; wine was all right, as long as no one drank too much of it—in case today ended up having the most cause for celebration.

The food, of course, was superb—*mon Dieu,* they were in Saint-Moritz, after all—and Tuck ate well, but did not overeat. Greg, however, went overboard on both food and wine; no one minded, because he wasn't on the team this year. Tuck found out Greg had nearly made the cut, but lost out by only one second to another teammate, Françoise. Excusing himself early, Tuck got back to his room before one a.m. He felt pleasantly tired, relaxed, and ready for sleep.

†

But during the night, Tuck had a strange dream, one that disturbed his deep sleep. He was skiing, very fast, down a mountain not unlike that which he had skied not twenty-four hours before. The snow melted under him, and became a road; the onlookers, wearing many colors that blurred into a purplish line as he skied past them at lightning speed, were all wearing white, and the background against which they stood was no longer a mountain, but a sort of stadium. It was an outdoor stadium, with rows and rows of bleachers, stretching up, up, up toward the sky. Tuck was no longer skiing; he was driving a low-slung sports car, painted in the French tricolors. Instead of a ski cap, he was wearing a helmet. As the car went faster and faster, he felt himself getting hotter and hotter, his head boiling inside the helmet. Taking one hand from the wheel, he tried to take the helmet off. He took both hands off the wheel in an effort to remove the helmet, in which his head was now melting, dripping like wax down, down, all over his racing outfit. The outfit also was too warm, and he tried desperately to take it off with his melted hands. A wall, a red and orange and yellow flame-y wall rushed at him, but he didn't care. He had to get out of that suit, out of that helmet, out of that car.

Tuck woke up, drenched in sweat, his heart being double-time. He took great gulps of air, trying to calm his racing pulse. He got out of bed, stumbling over the low table with his suitcase on it, trying to get to the bathroom. He switched on the light and lunged for the sink, turning on the cold tap and splashing, splashing, splashing his face, his arms, his torso. The face staring back at him with the terrified eyes was not red, as he imagined it would be, but ashen, drained of all color but gray. He placed his hands on either side of the sink, holding himself up, with his eyes closed, until he felt his heartbeat return to normal. Only then did he look at the man in the mirror; he was no longer ashen. Some color had returned to his cheeks—a red not unlike that of the dream wall toward which he had hurtled—and he shuddered.

†

In spite of the dream; in spite of losing so much sleep; Tuck won the gold at the 1948 Olympics. During the day of February 4th, the "madman of downhill" skied Val d'Isere to win the gold medal in both the men's downhill and slalom. On the night of February 4th, the champagne flowed, and this time, he drank whatever was put in front of him. Only twenty-two years old, he chose not, however, to enter another Olympics. Jean-Claud Killy had taken over Henrie's legend status.

Tuck was still obsessed with speed though. In 1952, he decided to become a race car driver, yet another sport at which he excelled. He won several titles, both in rallies and in racing, with the car he privately called *Zia*.

On October 7, 1962, Tuck, the "madman of downhill," was racing, sitting behind the wheel of his custom Ferrari *Zia*, when he began to feel warm—too warm. His head seemed to be on fire under his helmet. The dream he'd had in that Saint-Moritz hotel room came back to him in agonizing detail. Sweating, Tuck kept his hands on the wheel, willing himself to steady his breathing and not succumb to the feeling of melting flesh. He looked at his hands, which were gripping the wheel so tightly. *But they're not melting. It was only a dream, Tuck.* As he tried to breathe normally, his head seemed to cool down a little. *That's it. Steady now.* He took the next curve, slowing only slightly from his hundred-plus miles-per-hour speed.

Suddenly, it was as if a wall had dropped down in front of him; a red, orange, and yellow wall of flame. As he hurtled toward it, he involuntarily let go of the wheel, instinctively holding up both hands in front of his face to shield himself from the impact. The horrified crowd, watching from the rows and rows of bleacher-type seats in the Linas-Montlhéry autodrome, wondered why Oreiller veered off the track the way he did, when there was nothing there.

The world was told, in solemn accounts on both radio and the new invention, television, that Henrie Oreiller had died instantly, surrounded by the flaming wreckage of his beloved car. He was buried near Val d'Isere, next to his wife, and a shrine attesting to his sports prowess was erected in his honor.

†

And, one bright, cold day in October, exactly twenty years to the day Henrie was killed, a young American man visited Oreiller's grave. The man was a skier and long-time admirer of Oreiller, a young man his friends had nicknamed "the madman of downhill," after his skiing hero. As he read at the shrine about Oreiller's glory days on the slopes of Saint-Moritz, he allowed himself to dream. He thought that maybe, one day, he might ski to Olympic gold himself.

15

Ale

In heaven, there is no beer,
That's why we drink it here.
And when we're all gone from here
Our friends will be drinking all the beer.
"In Heaven There is No Beer"

Perfect. Tuck held the glass up to judge the color of its contents, then swirled the beer around, sniffing it appreciatively. *Heather and honey. It's coming through perfectly.* "Marc!" He called over his brew master. The tall, well-built man with the big dimples ambled over, a big grin on his face. "Marc, old son," said Tuck, clapping him on the shoulder, "this is a demm fine brew. I'm glad we nabbed you from the Danes before they realized what a treasure you are." He sniffed it first, then took a sip. "I think we just might make beer history with this batch."

"I tink so, too, George," smiled Marc. "What do ye tink ye'll call it den? 'Bow's Best'? or maybe 'Hodgson's Finest Hops'?" Marc gazed at the, what was at the time, abnormally pale liquid in the glass Tuck held in the air. "'Tis mighty pale, isn't it George?"

"Aye, 'tis."

"Well, we'll come up with a name for it, I warrant. We'll put our thinking caps on, maybe have a draft or two to help us in the creative process, and sleep on it." Tuck set the glass down on top of one of the big oak barrels. "But first, we need to make sure we get these first dozen barrels filled so that ship in the harbor has plenty for its voyage to India." He reached up and grabbed Marc's elbow, steering him in the direction of the Hodgson office. "No ship captain wants a boatload of thirsty sailors; they'll mutiny!" Tuck limped along next to the Dane towering above him.

Well, I'll be damned. Here I am walking next to a guy who looks like something out of Mel Brooks' Men In Tights. Okay, he isn't actually wearing tights, but I think I've got the right time period. Tuck took in the surrounding scene: the oak barrels, the stone walls of the brewery, the signs that said "Hodgson's Brewery: Purveyors of Fine Ales." *I may have landed in heaven. Okay, maybe they don't make Sierra Nevada, but they make beer, and it's my kind of beer.*

"I've thought of a name, Marc," he said. "What do you think of 'India Pale Ale'? We could call it 'IPA' for short." Tuck's eyes twinkled as he looked up at his brew master.

"I don't know, George, I'm sure." The Dane took off the brown cap he was wearing and scratched the head beneath the thick blond hair. "I don't know as it'll catch on sir, but ye can try it and see how she sails." Tuck gave a big laugh then, stretching up to cuff his friend on the shoulder. "I think that calls for a drink, Marc; I think that calls for a drink!"

"Won't your wife be waiting yer supper for ye? I don't want you to get in trouble, George." Marc's voice held a warning.

Damn. A wife? The way Marc's talking, I'd best have a drink before I face her anyway. "Eh. . . what did she say when you saw her last?" *That's a pretty innocent, non-committal kind of a question that shouldn't get me into too much trouble.* One look at the Dane's face, however, and he could see he should have asked a different question.

"But wasn't ye here when she came down dis afternoon?" Marc looked puzzled. "I didn't talk to her, like; you did, George. It's just she has such a loud voice and it carries a bit, and, well, I couldn't help overhearin'." Cap in hand still, Marc was looking everywhere but at Tuck.

"Ah, yes, yes. I must be losing the run of meself, Marc. Of course you're right. Came down, she did, right here, and started upbraiding me, of course, like she does…" Tuck could see he was digging himself a deeper hole.

"As a friend, even though you're my boss, George, I tink I need to say sometin' to ye." Marc cleared his throat, and looked toward the low, oak-beamed ceiling, hoping for inspiration. "Ye've been workin' too hard and ye need a rest, that's what I'm tinkin'." Marc said, all in a rush. "Ye've got the story all wrong, sir, and I tink you just need a rest." He took Tuck's arm and led him over to a set of stairs that climbed steeply into darkness. "Just go upstairs to the missus now, and I'll finish up down here." He put his cap back on, bowed stiffly, and turned away, shaking his head.

Okay. Guess I go up the stairs and see what's waiting for me. Marc must have seen Tuck's reluctance to ascend the stairs to who-knew-where. Before Tuck had even placed his foot on the bottom step, Marc was beside him again.

"George, I don't tink ye're in a fit state to go by yerself. I'm goin' wit ye." With that, the great Dane gently led Tuck up the twenty-five stairs to the home he had above the brewery. Marc knocked on the door—two quick taps—then opened it, calling out, "Oh missus Hodgson! I've a present for ye!"

Tuck could hear a woman's voice, increasing in volume as she gathered speed and sailed in their direction. "**Well he can't be drunk yet at this hour! What have you done this time, George Hodgson?**" As she hove into view, Tuck shrank back; he could feel Marc—all six-feet-six of him—shrink as well. *This is not going to be pretty.*

Tuck took in the details of the woman advancing rapidly toward him. *It's not so much that she's ugly.* Tuck studied her as closely as he dared. *She's sort of blown out of proportion. No, it's that she's got no proportion.* Only four feet, eight inches tall —at the most, he was being generous here—she was also approximately four feet, eight inches wide. She didn't have a mouth *per se*, it was a smear of off-red just above her chin, which, Tuck noted, had a wen with a single, long, black hair winding from it in a threatening way. As frightening as the red smear appeared when it was closed, Tuck soon realized he preferred it that way (for more than one reason; the first being its lack of volume control; surely he must be partially deaf by now?), for it managed to almost completely cover the few broken, plaque-covered teeth remaining in that fearsome maw.

Both men jumped back a couple of feet as She—Tuck daren't ask her name, and he didn't think she would either respond to or recognize an appellation like "darling"—advanced toward Tuck, in an effort to smell his breath. *She should try smelling her own. My God! I'll take beer breath any day.*

"As I suspected," she said, the smear pursing and emitting a sizeable *hmph*. "That's all you do down there is drink, George Hodgson. Why you couldn't have been a solicitor like you'd promised before we married, I don't know—"

Incredulous, Tuck's jaw dropped as Marc dared to stop the She in full flight. "Beggin' yer pardon, Kate," said Marc, drawing himself up to his full height in a vain attempt to cow the She, "but yer husband is feelin' poorly and that's why I've brought him to ye. He's been workin' hisself to the bone down there, and that's not the word of a lie, so help me—"

"*Don't* think of bringing *God* into this, Marc," she warned. Marc closed his mouth before he could get his foot any further into it. "Let's have a look at him," she said, her breath causing Tuck to nearly pass out. She poked his ample stomach, placed the back of her hand on his shoulder, felt his pulse, laid her greasy-haired, snow-white-capped head on his chest as if to hear his heart, and made him say *Ah-h-h-h* while she peered down his throat with her bulbous, rheumy eyes. "I see nothing a few leeches wouldn't fix straightaway. "Marc, go get Dr. Sitwell," she said dismissively. Seeing Marc made no move to go, she glared at him. "*Now* would be a lovely time to do so," she said, and turned away.

Marc still had made no move to go, and she turned her venomous eyes on him. "I can have your job, you know. GET DR. SITWELL *NOW*."

"It's just that, Ka—, I mean Mrs. Hodgson we've got to get an entire shipment of the new ale ready for the ship in the harbor and there's nothing wrong with Geor—, I mean, Mr. Hodgson dat a good lie-down won't cure and it'll make him feel worse if he gets bled and he won't be able to get the work done and I really *really* tink you should just let him be, so sorry, tankin' you Missus, and. . . and. . . I'll just go now bye." He paused only to catch his breath, then he disappeared through the doorway.

Kate was so stunned by Marc's outburst that she nearly forgot to scream at him. She remembered though, screaming down the staircase that he'd lose his job and what did he think he was, talking to her like that, and she was going to tell daddy, and other abusive comments that merely bounced off Marc's retreating form.

Tuck, for his part, thought *That man has balls.* He looked at his wife. *And I think she took the ones I had.* He sighed. Kate took this as a personal affront and turned to attack him instead, or at least that's what he thought.

Instead, she coyly grinned, her jagged fangs flashing dully within the red smear, in what she must have thought was a winsome smile. "*Well* my sweet," the word coming out like *fweet*, "that's taken care of that great Danish *oaf* for a while, anyway." She sidled closer and began to unbutton, first his waistcoat, then his shirt. With her great greasy head, she nested happily into the hollow above Tuck's great paunch. "I thought you would *nev*er come home," she sighed. Then she giggled, the sound somewhere between an owl's screech and an out-of-tune violin. "Imagine leeching you when all you need is a bit of slap-and-tickle!"

I'd rather have the leeches, if it's all the same to you. Tuck considered running out the door and following Marc. Quickly—more quickly than he dreamed she could move, except that she was a woman with a mission—the greasy head came unstuck from his chest, her right hand grabbed his left and he was dragged out of the tiny kitchen into what he could only hope was not the bedroom. *Nope. It's the bedroom. Luckily it's pretty dark in here.* He watched the blurred waddle as she quick-marched him into the bedchamber. *It just can't be dark enough. Why did I not drink more beer before I came up here? I could have used 'brewer's droop' as an excuse.* He resigned himself to his duty and shed his clothes, but not nearly as rapidly as She did.

To his surprise, after he got in bed and she covered him with kisses, he was able to perform quite admirably. *Obviously old George rather likes the She. They must do this a lot.* As she laid in contented silence (*ah, that's why he does it—the silence afterward, the merciful silence*), draped over his short, rotund body, he smoked the pipe he'd found on the small oak table beside the massive feather bed. *Well. That wasn't bad. There's no such thing as bad sex, only sex that's too short or too long,* Tuck mused, waxing philosophical. *Now if I can just keep her in the dark, I'll be fine...*

They jumped, startled, at the *knock-knock* on their front door. "Missus Hodgson, it's me, Marc, back with the leeches."

"Oh *dear*,' whispered She, "*did* I remember to lock the *door*?"

Her question was answered only a few seconds later, when Tuck and Kate saw Marc's large frame looming in the entrance to the bedroom. Marc was so shocked at seeing Kate and Tuck together naked, Tuck was not surprised when the jar holding the leeches crashed to the floor. Marc's huge frame was the next thing to hit the floor, as Marc toppled as well.

I'm not surprised. Poor Marc. I can only imagine what we look like to him. She, meanwhile, had sprung out of bed and run over to Marc. Her huge, saggy breasts brushed Marc's back as she tried to roll him over, or at least move him enough to feel his pulse. Tuck watched, fascinated, as he watched her struggle mightily.

"George, for *god's* sake, would you get *over* here this *mi*nute! I don't think he's *breathi*ng."

With that, Tuck leaped out of bed himself. "Get some clothes on, woman," he barked. "Marc! Marc!" Tuck rolled him over with difficulty, and then blanched when he saw Marc's face. It had leeches all over it, and jagged pieces of glass stuck out at odd angles—one in his eye, one in his cheek, and—Tuck choked back a sob—in his neck. The chunk of glass had severed the jugular vein, and blood was spurting from Marc's neck. She had returned from putting a dressing gown over her naked self, and she bent down, placing her hand on Tuck's shoulder.

"Does he have a pulse?" she asked, knowing what the answer would be. She, too, had seen the blood, which was forming a slowly spreading stain under Mark's body, reaching to the hem of Kate's dressing gown and pooling around Tuck's knees.

"I don't think so, my sweet," said Tuck, his fingers removing gently the shard and then closing the eyes of his brew master. He attempted to remove the leeches, too, but Kate's hand, softly placed on Tuck's, stopped him.

"I'll do that, luv," she said. "You go get yourself dressed, and I'll take care of Marc."

†

The funeral was held two days later. Tuck bought a fine headstone, intending to have it engraved with Marc's full name. He had trouble finding that out, though, as paperwork was not as important to a brewer as it would have been to a solicitor. Searching through the papers Tuck found in Marc's small bedsit, he saw what looked like a page torn out of a church registry. *Well this will have to do.* Tuck didn't know any Danish, but the birth date was clear enough: "*8 Dec. 1753. Boy to M. and Ms. Jakobsen, Marcus Z.*"

"Oh! Zia!" was all Tuck said, before collapsing into sobs.

16

Ship's Wreck

...they forgot I wasn't really a captain, we were all commercials together.
...I'd only heard the noise over the roofs and seen the screens tremble.
Graham Greene, England Made Me

The ship pitched and careened, knocking Tuck off balance and sending him crashing against the ship's rail. Squinting against the driving, horizontal, ice-needle rain, he had trouble seeing further than his own hands. He couldn't tell if the crew—those that were left after the mutiny—was on deck or not; surely they wouldn't abandon the *Zia* now, in her hour of need? He got to his feet cautiously, keeping his leather-gloved hands against the side of the ship, feeling his way as the boat arced and dipped with sickening irregularity, counting, in a half-whisper, *One foot, two feet, three feet, three-and-a-half; rail should be here now—it is! Grip it tightly with both hands, Tuck. Now, make for the mast!*

†

The fifty-two foot schooner had not been built for the rough ocean; it was meant for the calmer waters that sponges preferred to inhabit. The boat had drifted far from its intended course and was now far from the Greek island port from which it had sailed. Tuck owned this boat, which took the sponge divers—proud Greek men from the island of Kalymnos—out to the deep waters of the Aegean. There the men, without benefit of diving suits or any gear save their incredible courage and a special knife, would tie a rope around their waists, clench the knife tightly between their teeth, and dive for the precious sponges whose by-products were craved by Europeans and Americans alike.

Competition for sponges was fierce; the waters Tuck normally sailed to for the sponge harvest now hosted many boats—American, British, Portuguese—and many greedy captains willing to sacrifice their divers in their quest for the versatile sponge. Sponges were used for everything from contraceptive devices to surgical dressings to fancy bath items.

Most of the "captains" on the other ships knew very little about sailing. Tuck, however, had been in the Royal Navy, that is, until he was court-martialed for something he couldn't remember doing. The potent grog on the Indonesian island on which they had been getting a little shore time had gotten the better of Tuck, or so his commanding officer had told him at the trial.

Tuck needed a job after the court martial, but the only life he had known or cared about was the sea. He had seen the demand for sponges increase a thousand-fold, and he also knew the Kalymnos islanders were the best in the world at getting them. Scraping together what little money he had managed not to drink while in His Majesty's Service, he bought a schooner, repaired it expertly, shanghaied a few recruits from a filthy East London pub, and headed for Greece.

The day he arrived at Kalymnos, he was in luck: a tropical storm had destroyed most of the Greek divers' usual transport, and they were in need of a ship to take them out so they could ply their trade. It was the only way they knew to keep their families fed; in two days, the divers could earn enough to keep their families fed for a month. Tuck had no problem conscripting fifteen men for his venture. After a week in the glorious island sun, he was ready to take the *Zia* out; Tuck was going to be an independent merchant in the sponge trade.

The first two days, still within sight of Kalymnos, the fifteen divers duly brought up enough sponges to keep them financially viable for a month, including Tuck. Tuck wanted more, however: he was a greedy man. Other ships were starting to arrive, having heard somehow that this spot was the best, probably from islanders talking to those on the mail boats that plied their way from island to island every week. He ordered his few English-speaking crew members to venture further out. They refused. They didn't like the look of the islanders on board, whose language they could not understand, but whose looks said, *We want to go home now.*

Tuck took his shanghaied crew aside, one by one. "Listen, matey. This ship is going out to the Pacific—with or without you. If you choose not to obey orders, then I will choose to slit your throat when you are asleep. And sleep you will—with the fishes—for I shall throw you overboard and you'll never see England again." With that, Tuck would draw his knife, ever so lightly, across the man's throat, enough to draw blood, but not to kill him. Using this technique, he was able to keep his crew; the Greeks were another matter, however.

They, too, were skillful with knives—far more so than Tuck—and they outnumbered the crew. They saw what was happening after Tuck had a "conversation" with an Englishman, and decided they needed to take matters into their own hands. In the early hours of the fourth day out at sea, they huddled under and near a stack of sails and ropes in the boat's stern, certain that Tuck, at least, was sleeping. They had given him their special liquor, ouzo, of which "Captain Tuck" was over-fond, as well as giving some ouzo as a bribe to the crew members whose watch it was.

The Greek leader, sitting on his haunches and addressing his fellows in a low, earnest voice, heard the footstep too late. After one swift, silent stroke, his severed head rolled to one side, bouncing against the ropes and, as the boat dipped, rolled toward the stairs leading to the galley. The Greek's leader was not the only one to die. Five other men, too, met their deaths as Tuck's men emerged from the lifeboats, which were beside the Greek meeting place, moments after the leader had been dispatched.

The Greeks, shocked at what had happened to their friends and fellow divers, nonetheless responded quickly, unsheathing their knives and killing three of Tuck's men. But the element of surprise was the deciding factor. In moments, it was all over: the rest of the Greeks, except the two who had warned Tuck of the intended mutiny, were bound together securely until daylight, when, one by one, their throats were slit and they were thrown overboard. Their countrymen, the two that were left, could do nothing but watch and think silent prayers for their friends.

Now Tuck had a real dilemma: although he knew a little about the Pacific, he had only been a skivvy when he had been out on the ocean before. He had neither captained a ship, nor steered it himself, and the one shanghaied sailor who had known anything had been knifed to death by a mutineer. The schooner had drifted dangerously off course during the course of the ouzo-filled night and the resulting massacre, and Tuck frankly did not know where he was, except that they were on the open seas, and no other ships could be seen, no matter which direction he looked through his telescope. He would have to hope for a clear night to try and determine his course by the stars.

It was not to be.

†

The ship groaned as it tossed upon the waves. Tuck knew the ship was angry at him for murdering thirteen men. *But they were against me!* He could barely make out some moving shapes—*are those my crew members? Good-for-nothings!* Tuck wrapped his right arm around the mast and gesticulated with his left hand at the frightened men scurrying to safety.

He shouted, the wind whipping his words into the maelstrom, "Go down if you like, you lily-livered *SISSIES!*" He had to use both arms on the mast as the storm increased in intensity, tossing the boat starboard. "That's right! Run away, you *COWARDS!* What was I thinkin', lettin' you sail with me!

Cowards and good-for-nothings! Yer a disgrace to this ship! Yer a disgrace to me! Me!!!! The finest ship's captain you will ever sail with!"

The ship pitched and tossed, but Tuck clung bravely to the mast, laughing maniacally. "Ha-ha! Hee-hee!" He caught one of the men staring at him, wide-eyed, unable to move, frozen. "What're you starin' at, you old fool! Stop lookin' at me!!"

Above the wind's howl; above the sound of the crashing waves; Tuck heard a voice call to him, as if from far, far away. He stopped his haranguing; listening with all his might, squinting his eyes as if that would help him hear better, he tried hard—so hard—to place the voice. *Where's that voice coming from? Is that my ship? Is that you, my Zia? What're you saying?*

"I can't hear you! Speak up!!!"

"I said," the bus driver called over his shoulder, "this is your stop. Didn't you want Seventh and Hawthorne?"

Tuck unsquinted his eyes. Everyone on the crowded bus stared at him, wide-eyed, unable to move, frozen. Tuck was still clinging, with both hands, to the yellow pole by the bus's front exit. He could feel that his pants were wet where he'd peed himself, but he didn't touch it to make sure. He was pretty sure. He hoped his bright yellow sou'wester was covering it. Removing his right hand from the yellow pole, he saluted the bus driver.

"Thank you very much, captain." He gave a small bow. "This is indeed my stop."

And Tuck lurched off the bus.

17

Sacrifice

Digging in the dirt

to find the places I got hurt.

Peter Gabriel, "Digging in the Dirt"

With the fine camel's hair brush, Tuck swept away the accumulated dirt and dust that had filled the cracks of the engraved urn. "Hey! You guys!" he called excitedly. "Look at this!"

The two team members closest to him, Leah and Adrienne, came running, stepping lightly and gracefully over the small mounds of earth at the dig.

"What have you found, Chief?" Leah asked, breathless with excitement. "Have we struck pay dirt?"

"I think so." He carefully brushed away more of the dirt. "Look at the inscription. If that isn't Mayan, I don't know what is." He looked up at Adrienne. "What do you think? You're the language expert."

Adrienne adjusted her glasses and put her nose almost on top of the urn. "Yep, that's Mayan." She sat on her haunches, her elbows resting lightly on her knees, her hands dangling between them. "If I'm right, this site is going to be about seven thousand years old." She looked at Leah. "What about the artwork? I can see orange and ochre on that clay; maybe some blue, but it's hard to tell with only the small bit that's showing. What do you think?"

It was Leah's turn to peer closely at the buried object. "Hmm. I'll have to see more of it than that." She asked Tuck, "Do you want us to help you with this? With the three of us working on it, we can have it out of there by sunset." All three of them looked up at the mountain towering directly before them, where the sun was just beginning to dip below its crest.

"As exciting as this is, I think we should leave it, ladies." Tuck scanned the dig site for the two other members of his team. "I'd like the others to be in on this, for one thing. But I also want to be sure we take our time. It looks like an intact sample, the first one we've come across. I don't want us to have to rush this, and I don't want to have to dig by search light, either. This has to be done right." The women nodded their agreement with Tuck's rationale. "We may have just found us—quite literally—a gold mine."

They decided to rope off the area and cover it with a tarp, in case the weather turned bad during the night. The changeable Andes weather, especially in the valley where they were staying, between rainforests and high deserts, would erupt into downpours with no warning. The effect of these sudden rains was sometimes beneficial: more than one valuable relic had been found after the rain had washed away a layer of soil they had not yet penetrated. More often, however, the intensity of the rain ruined what had been earth-protected for thousands of years, and the archaeologists would watch as precious shards joined the rivulets that eventually became the mighty Amazon. Because they couldn't carry enough tarp with them to cover every site, they had to guess which one might hold treasures that needed protecting.

This time it was easy, though: they knew they had found treasure, and protected it accordingly. After securing the tarp, made of a lightweight parachute silk, the three of them made their way back to camp, across the clearing where the site was, about half a mile through thick forest.

Tuck was the first to reach his tent, one of three they had pitched in a small space in the forest. Tuck's was smaller than the other two, because it was only for him; there was one large tent for the women to share, and one large one for the two men, Carlos and Kevin. "*Wee*-ooo!" Tuck sing-songed their special signal, something the mimicking birds native to this region would not copy. "*Wee*-ooo! Carlos? Kev?" Calling over his shoulder, he yelled, "Hey, Leah; Adrienne! Take a look for those guys, wouldja? They should be back by now."

Although technically a forest, it felt more like a jungle, the deciduous and coniferous trees at this four thousand foot level holding as many different types of animals, snakes, and spiders in their branches as any jungle—and they were just as dangerous, especially after dark.

And it was getting darker by the minute. The sun was no longer visible behind the neighboring mountain, only a vivid red-orange streak gradating, however faintly, into all the colors of the rainbow. Tuck set about lighting fires in the semi-permanent pits strategically placed around the perimeter of the campsite. It was still the best way to keep wild animals at bay during the night, they'd found. Each fire had its own sort of metal umbrella so even if it rained, the fire would not go out; one of the marvels of modern science they could enjoy even here, so far from civilization.

The women had returned, Leah carrying a basket full of the berries and nuts they used to supplement the dehydrated foods they had brought with them. They were all vegetarians, except Carlos, who occasionally shot something for his dinner, cooking it on a spit over the fire.

"Well, we didn't see them out there at all, Chief," said Leah, dumping the berries and nuts onto the camp table outside Tuck's tent. "What do you think's happened to them?"

"Did you actually check their tent?" Adrienne started walking toward it. "Maybe they knocked off early and came back to take a nap."

"Would *you* be able to sleep if I was giving our signal?" Tuck said, shrugging his shoulders. "Personally, I think I do it loud enough to wake the dead, let alone those two sleeping slackers." He sat in one of the camp's lightweight folding chairs, cracking open hazelnuts one by one, and popping them into his mouth.

Adrienne considered for a moment, then decided to check the tent anyway. "Maybe you're not as loud as you think you are, or they're more tired than they thought they were. I'll just go check."

Just then, a huge gust of wind whipped through the camp, upsetting the table and its contents, and blowing the chairs, except for the one Tuck sat in, across the clearing.

"Whoa-a-a-! What was *that*?! Leah. . . Adrienne. . . are you guys okay?" Leah had been next to the fire when the gust came, and it took her by surprise, causing her to trip and nearly land, hands down, in the fire pit. Adrienne had been pushed backward from the door of the tent, the gust was so strong, and she had landed on the ground.

"Yes, fine," the girls chorused.

"But barely," said Leah. "That was close! I nearly became a sacrifice!" She laughed merrily. "Of course, the Great God requires a virgin for that, and, ah—"

"Yeah, Leah, we get the point," Adrienne's eyebrows lifted and she teased, "you haven't qualified as one of those for about ten years now, have you?"

"Ha bloody ha!" Leah gave Adrienne a playful push. "But of course, it takes one to kn—"

"Jesus, girls, will ya lay off?" Both girls turned to look at Tuck, and he saw the look of surprise on their faces at the tone of his voice. He softened it a bit, saying, "Sorry. It's just that I'm worried about Carlos and Kevin. There's no reason for them not to be here." One glance at their faces, and he could see that they were worried, too. All three of them instinctively took a step or two closer to the others.

"Okay, we all know this area's history—its dangerous animals, its myths, and whatnot—but I think I should also remind us that Carlos and Kevin are extremely capable and know how to handle themselves out here." Tuck motioned the women over to the table, righting the blown-over chairs so they'd have a place to sit. Sitting around the table, the firelight dancing on their faces, Tuck opened a pack of dried apricots and offered some to Leah and Adrienne, which they took. Munching thoughtfully, Tuck said, "Okay, let's think about this. We might've been spooked by finding the camp empty and then the wind gust coming along, but let's look at facts." The women nodded. "Where are the men most likely to be?"

Leah spoke first. "Well, they were working on that site just over the rise from us, about—what?—a quarter of a mile away, at most. Remember, where we found the dolman?" She took another bite of apricot, then said, "It's conceivable that they, like we, found something incredible, and decided to keep at it until they finished. They could have camped there for the night even."

"But did they have their gear with them?" asked Adrienne. "They sure didn't have it with them this morning when we left camp."

"They could have come back and got it, though," said Tuck. "Don't forget, their site is that much closer to camp then ours is, and it would have been easy for them to pop back over here to get their gear."

"I can go check their tent, Chief," said Leah. "At least we'll know if that's what happened, if their stuff is gone."

"Good idea," said Tuck. "Do you want us to come along—moral support?"

"No, no. I'll be fine. You're right here! What can happen to me in the fifteen feet to their tent?" She left the table, taking out her flashlight and turning it on as she sprinted over. She parted the tent's flaps, carefully directed the flashlight over the interior, then snapped the light off. She turned back to them, calling out as she walked, "The stuff's gone. No tents, no gear left in there. It's as neat as a pin," she grinned, "which is more than I can say for *our* tent, Adrienne!"

More relieved than he wanted to let on, Tuck said, "Well, that mystery's solved then. They decided to make camp at the dig. Great! We can all go to bed." He got up. "Who's got first watch? Is it me?"

"Nope, Chief, it's me."

"Okay, Leah. Thanks. See you in the morning."

"Throw something at me to wake me up, Leah, or I won't get up on time for the watch, okay?" Adrienne yawned and headed toward their tent. "I'm bushed. 'Night all."

"Good night, you two. Don't let those famous bedbugs bite."

†

That night, Tuck dreamed he was walking toward a rise, a large one, in the distance. He was by himself, dressed in lightweight brown clothes, of a material he'd never felt before. It was smooth against his skin, like suede, yet it was airy; this he knew because although the day was hot, he did not feel uncomfortable. There was a sun—he couldn't tell if it was on its way up or down, in front of him, to the left of the rise. Although there were some tall hills—not quite mountains—further away, the rise toward which he headed was the tallest thing around him on the brownish plain across which he traveled, an undergrowth with smallish shrubs that had branches that scratched his ankles. His ankles were bare, as were his feet, apart from the skin of leather hide, soft and supple, strapped lightly through his first and second toes with a thin piece of rope.

He ran closer to the mound. It looked from a distance as if it had a toupee on it, a mat of hair, curled and tight and dark capping two-thirds of the head that was the rise itself. As Tuck began his ascent of the mound, he could see that the mat was really more of the same undergrowth through which he'd come, but closer together and at a different stage of growth, as if it were dying, or had been scorched by fire. The black, crisp tendrils slowed his progress, clinging to him as if they did not want him to go any further.

Tuck was looking for something—an entrance—but everything looked the same. It was difficult to detect any difference in the uniformity confronting him, the black, rooty plants first luring him closer, then holding him fast. He managed to get to the top of the rise, and he looked back from whence he'd come. For miles and miles, the unchanging landscape stretched before his gaze. The other side of the rise, now that he was up here and could get a good look, appeared exactly the same as the side up which he'd scrambled. There was a mountain behind him, and far, far away on the other side of the rise, he could see the glint of what might be a river, but other than that was nothing but the strange scrub brush. Had he come all that way, across the desolate, barren landscape, all by himself? He did not feel tired, nor did he feel thirsty, yet he had nothing with him but a small pouch, a leather pouch, strapped around his waist. At this point, he looked inside it.

He struggled with the leather strings, so tightly tied together. For a moment, he hesitated: perhaps his strength came from within it, and he would be wrong to open it. After a pause, he decided to open it anyway. It seemed the right thing to do. His thick, calloused fingers nonetheless were patient, and he dexterously pried the two leather strings apart.

As he opened the bag, the earth opened below his feet, and he dropped—not in a frightening way, but gently and speedily, into the rise, landing on his leather-clad feet on a smooth-topped, huge boulder inside a cavernous space. The earth closed over his head—he saw the oval of sky grow smaller and smaller—but it was still light inside, not bright, but light enough to see the cave walls; to see that he stood on the wide, smooth boulder; to see that there was a sort of viaduct, empty of water, immediately in front of him. The air was fresh and clean-smelling, not earthy or damp. Searching for the source of the light, he noticed, all along the walls, that there were recesses in which a stone—about the size of an orange, and glowing its color—was placed, and from which emitted the radiant light softly falling about him. His boulder abutted the cave wall behind him; he walked over to the recess on that wall, intending to pick up the stone and examine it.

As he reached toward it, however, a current of electricity arced toward his fingers, shocking him sufficiently so that he withdrew his hand quickly. He could feel heat emanating from it, and realized that was why the cave was so pleasant inside, not cold at all.

But where was the breeze coming from? Walking to the edge of the boulder, near the viaduct, he could feel, from his right, a wonderful breeze, cool and refreshing. It seemed to be the source of the pure, sweet air he was breathing. Looking in the direction from which the breeze was coming, he could not see much, as the viaduct curved around further to the right and was lost in darkness as it rounded his boulder, rising gently upward and away from him in what he guessed was a spiral; for as he looked left, he noticed that the viaduct sloped gently downwards, losing itself in the curve, and all becoming dark again, maybe twenty yards from where he stood.

Just then he heard a rushing sound—water? Tuck wasn't afraid; it wasn't a frightening sound *per se*; he was just curious. The breeze stiffened; the rushing sound increased in intensity. Tuck strained to see what was coming from his right. Suddenly the water gushed from the opening, sweeping Tuck off his feet and hurtling him along the viaduct. The water was deep, far deeper than he had imagined, and he tumbled and somersaulted in the water's delicious coolness. He soon realized he could lie on his back, as if he were on an inner tube (just like he used to do as a child on the Apple River back home), and travel, feet first, down the rushing cataract, as if he were *part* of the cataract.

Down the water spiraled, Tuck one with the water, in pure enjoyment, when it abruptly stopped, and he found himself treading water in the deep pool into which the cataract had dumped him. The water glowed greenly from more of the strange stones he could see deep, deep down in the pool—twenty, thirty feet or more. The water was body temperature, just perfect, and it was so clear that he could see the recesses in which the stones sat. The pool was not that wide—maybe twenty feet at most, but he could not see its bottom. It seemed to taper into a small hole, but it could have been a trick of the light and the depth combined.

Tuck could see the opening where the cataract had tumbled; he could see, ahead of him and slightly to his left, a boulder similar to the one from which he'd come: or was it the same one? He pondered this, treading water, the only sound being the *tish. . .tish. . .tish. . .* of his still-leather-clad feet in the deep pool, his hands waving—forward and back, forward and back—silently, slowly, in the pristine pool.

At length he saw, as he paddled around the pool, steps carved into the stone boulder. At first he wondered why he hadn't noticed them before, then realized it was because he was seeing the boulder from a different angle. He climbed out of the water, taking each step carefully, water puddling in his wake. The stone steps were small, tiny even, only big enough for one of his feet at a time, and only the ball of his foot would fit. The steps, too, spiraled up; perhaps it was because the steps were so tiny that it seemed to take forever to get to the top of the boulder; it was almost as if the top of the rock receded as he took each step. He could not hurry, for he was afraid he'd fall back, into the pool below. As pleasant a prospect as that was, he sensed he could no longer go back; he needed to move forward and upward.

Though his clothes were no longer wet from the pool, now a long way down, the effort of the climb had caused Tuck to sweat profusely, and he found his clothes soaked again. It also made the last hundred or so steps slippery, and, looking down at the watery chasm, he was glad he had not slipped and landed in it. From this height it was not so much inviting as frightening. He marveled at how far he'd come.

The summit of this boulder was much different than the one he'd found himself at the beginning of his descent into the rise; this was not, after all, his starting place. If anything, it looked like an ending place: it had a sort of altar, surrounded by a trough (probably for the blood that would have gushed from a sacrificed animal, he thought); there was a dolman, taller than he was; and there was a pile of carefully heaped, small stones, covering, almost like a small mountain range, a rectangular spot about four feet long and two feet wide. It resembled a cairn more than anything.

The altar abutted the stone wall of the cave and was directly in front of him; Tuck explored it with his hands and discovered the altar had been formed out of the rock wall itself. The dolman was to his left, standing alone, majestic, its vertical stones about four feet high, with a smallish quoit between two and three feet thick atop it, and the stone cairn was to his right. Around the dolman and cairn was grass—green, verdant. The altar stood on the bare rock, rock incapable of sustaining any life. Tuck laid his two hands on the altar and closed his eyes. He felt a current run through his limbs, right down to his toes; in his trance, he heard the cries of a woman resound against the stone walls, cries of agony and pain. Quickly, still in the dream, he opened his eyes and lifted his hands from the warm stone. Both the current and the cries ended. Testing, he placed his hands back on the stone; again, he heard the cries and felt the electricity run through him. He kept his hands there this time, though, and a vision came to him.

A woman. Long, dark hair; thick. Beautiful. Soft, full breasts. Skirt—no, pelts. Long, soft. Pouch around her waist, leather. Lying on altar. Crying! Hand reaching, child's hand reaching, fingertips touching. Tuck jumped as a huge knife, seemingly in his own hands, or held by someone in his own body, slit the beautiful woman from neck to groin. Blood, so much blood. Woman still crying. Voice. Man's. 'Zia, you will die. You must die.' Man crying. Child screaming. Tuck forced himself to stay in the spot until the vision ended. Heart. Ripped out. Still beating.

Tuck opened his eyes in the dream, his eyes wet with tears. *"Zia!"* he cried.

His dream cry woke Tuck. He found himself in his tent in the remote Andes valley, dark and alone, still full of the bloody vision, and he shuddered under his Thinsulate blanket.

He found he was no longer able to sleep, though he tossed and turned for a while. Why had Adrienne not woken him for his watch? Perhaps it was too early for his shift; he would go out and relieve whoever was on duty at the moment. He quickly slipped into his clothes, doing it easily in the dark from long practice, and he left the tent.

All was quiet in the clearing. *Too quiet. Where was Leah? or Adrienne?* He called out softly their names in turn. "Leah!" Silence. "Adrienne!" Silence again. Scanning the area, he could see none of the fires had gone out, and everything looked exactly as it had when he went to bed. *Who was supposed to be on watch, and where was she?*

As if in answer, he heard the sound of a Velcro strip on a tent door opening quickly, and Leah, yawning, wearing her pajamas, stuck the top half of herself out of the tent flap. "What's up, Chief?" she asked, sleepily.

"Sorry to wake you, Leah," apologized Tuck. "I couldn't sleep— and my watch has stopped, so have no idea what time it is, either—and so thought I'd relieve whoever was on duty." He looked ruefully at her. "Apparently, it's not you, is it? Sorry to wake you." He added, "But where's Adrienne, then? Is she in there?" Tuck indicated the tent, and Leah shook her head.

"No, I don't think so." Her head disappeared into the tent and popped back out again. "Nope." She scratched her nose and yawned again. "She came out for her watch before I'd had a chance to wake her." Big yawn. "Wow, it's still really dark, isn't it? What time is it?" She paused. "Oh, that's right; you said your watch isn't working. That's funny, Chief," she added, "mine isn't either. It stopped after that big gust of wind last night. Is that when yours went out?"

"No," Tuck answered. "I noticed mine had stopped when we were out at the site yesterday, right about the time we made the find." They looked at each other, eyebrows raised. "Significant? Probably not; just a coincidence. Who knows." He waved her back inside, saying, "Don't worry about anything, Leah. I'll find Adrienne. You go back to sleep."

"Righty-o, Chief. Thanks."

Tuck decided to check every square inch of the camp site before starting to worry about Adrienne—even if the whole camp couldn't have been more than fifty feet by fifty feet or thereabouts. Methodically, he started at the perimeter, peering into the bushes and flashing his lights up and down the trees that bordered it. He walked in an ever-decreasing circle, making sure he covered all the ground outside the tents. Nothing. *No Adrienne, anyway.* The only thing that seemed different was a spot, near the path they used for egress and ingress, where the undergrowth was flattened as if something had been dragged through there. He hadn't noticed it before, but then again, it was so close to the path that it may have been caused by one of them setting down something heavy, or bringing in an extra load of either firewood or food.

He was reluctant to follow the path further, not wanting to leave the safety of the fire circle. It was still too dark to see anything. He looked in the sky for a hint of daylight, but only the stars in the clear sky winked back.

First, Carlos and Kevin. Now Adrienne. Who was next? And where had they gone? There was no sign of bloodshed or foul play. They had just *vanished.* Tuck's scientific mind knew there had to be a rational explanation. Then he remembered his strange dream. *That* didn't seem too rational.

He returned to the center of the camp site, rejuvenated the fire, and made himself some coffee. He sprinkled some of his tobacco-weed mixture into the paper made by a Peruvian tribe and rolled himself a joint. He smoked contemplatively, sipping his coffee and watching as the first tentative fingers of dawn scratched the night sky. He forgot all about who was missing, or why, as he sat there on the silvery folding camp chair, appreciating—not for the first time—the native's reverence for their Sun God. He thought how they must have felt—relieved, joyful, thankful—when they saw the Sun make His appearance after a long and dark night. Tuck's mind drifted, thinking not only of the Sun's rise, but of its setting, and of their rituals, and of their sacrifices—

With a start, Tuck snapped back to the present. *Sacrifice. What we found yesterday wasn't a gold mine. It was a place of sacrifice, of burial, of death.* He remembered the cairn and the dolman and the altar, the three things from his dream, and he suddenly saw, in his mind's eye, how it matched the configuration of the dig, the site they had tarped over yesterday: *it was the rise I saw in my dream.* He was anxious for sunrise now. He just knew they'd discover the altar, the dolman, and the cairn at the dig. And the rushing stream dream! Near the camp site was the stream of pure, cold water from the towering mountain beside him now, the mountain from behind whose topmost peak the sun was gracefully rising. He couldn't wait to tell the others.

Excitedly, he ran to the women's tent, calling before entering, "Leah! Leah! I know what's at the dig! We've got to get down there, *now.*" He whipped the tent flap aside, hearing the Velcro's loud *r-r-r-r-r-reeeeech.*

A quick look at the disheveled pile of clothing and open sleeping bags showed Tuck that she was not inside. "Damn. Where'd *she* go?" He closed the flap more carefully than he had opened it; no one liked to find, curled up in the bedclothes, a curious snake who had found easy access into the tent. He was going to head to his own tent and gather what he thought he might need, but a thought came to him, an irrational one, that Leah might be in the men's tent for some reason. Again calling her name before entering, he undid the opening— which he noticed had the extra storm flaps done up, from the outside—and stepped in.

Involuntarily, he retched. The scene in front of him was ghastly: both Carlos and Kevin were dead. They had been slit from throat to groin, and again from nipple to nipple and likewise from hip to hip across the abdomen, and both men had been castrated. They were laid out in such a way that their feet were touching, their hands and arms outstretched in a crucifix-like manner. Under each naked body was a tarp, the same kind Tuck had used to cover the dig site. There were crudely made candles, small, varied in color and shape, placed in a circle around the bodies every twelve inches, forming what looked like a macabre sort of zodiacal motif. In spite of the mountain heather placed in between the candles and strewn over the bodies, no attempt had been made to embalm the bodies, and they were beginning to reek. Heather, being a natural pest repellent, had at least kept the bodies falling prey to the multitude of insect life that would otherwise have destroyed them.

Now it was even more imperative for Tuck to find the women, to protect them from the crazed man or monster that could do such evil to two members of his team. Tuck didn't know what to do with the men's bodies; maybe he'd better just leave them for now. "You won't be going anywhere, will you," he said softly. "I'll find who did this to you, I promise." Tuck turned on his heel and left the stench of the tent, closing the Velcro flap with care. "Someone knew enough to close that flap up tightly," he said aloud. "And that looks like a very human thing to do."

Entering his own tent, the first thing he saw was that his sleeping bag had been neatly rolled up, and his gear had been packed, ready to go. *When did this happen? I was only a few feet away the entire time, either checking the perimeter or sitting right outside the goddamn tent. This is impossible. . . unless—*

Maybe he *had* packed it up himself and had just forgotten. Maybe he'd smoked too much weed, and it caused him to forget—this South American stuff was extremely powerful. *Stop it. There's a reason for everything, including this.* He was starting to doubt his sanity.

He quickly checked the contents of the backpack to be sure it really contained all the things he thought he might need. If he'd packed it while under the influence of drugs, he might have missed something. It looked all right, but, just in case, he would refill the water bottle with fresh water from the stream. Giving the tent one last scan, he left, closing the flap as carefully as he had the other two, then he dashed to the stream, emptying the bottle as he ran.

The sun was inching toward its midpoint in the sky, although it wasn't noon yet. It was probably about nine or ten a.m. For some reason unknown to him, he knew he must get to the dig before noon. He paused at the camp's perimeter next to the path, only to see if, now that it was daylight, he would be able to detect how far the flattened grass extended. His heart sank as he saw that it followed alongside the path exactly, only disappearing when a tree stump or boulder was in the way. And he noticed that on that on each stump or boulder was blood. He quickened his steps, ducking whenever a low-hanging branch came his way. He felt as if the forest itself were trying to prevent him from reaching the dig site. *Please don't let me be too late*, he breathed, though he did not know what he might be "too late" for.

Tuck tried, as he ran, to see how far the sun had risen; it was in vain, as the dense, overhanging trees effectively blocked his vision. Finally, after what seemed to Tuck like an hour, but was probably only fifteen or twenty minutes, he broke through the last of the brush. There, before him, was the dig, the site that had turned up the engraved urn he and the women had left behind yesterday. And, he realized, he was no longer alone.

The first thing to attract his attention was that the tarp had been removed. It was now on top of the rise, spread out in a circle, and looking like a white sun. The second thing he noticed, with a sick feeling in the pit of his stomach, was that Adrienne's body was lying, not in the middle, but, from Tuck's vantage point, at about the three o'clock mark of the tarp. She was cut open like Carlos and Kevin; she, too, was naked, with her arms outstretched like the others' had been.

The third thing he heard first, and saw a moment later: as the underbrush crackled behind him, he heard the *swoosh* of a machete, and as he turned, he saw how Leah's long, thick black hair framed her maniacal face—just before she sliced him in two, from top to bottom, screaming "For Teosinte!"

†

It was to be another twenty years before anyone else ventured into this part of the rainforest. Burning had begun years before, as the makers of cheap hamburgers needed ever more acreage for their poorly treated cows to feed from. Greenpeace had sent an advance party to see if they could find anything,

anything at all, to stop the giant corporations' advances on the pristine area. What the party found stunned them, and caused the bulldozers to stop in their tracks.

Evidence of the sacrificial rites performed twenty years earlier were still visible, in particular, the large tarp, no longer white, but still visible under the mounds covered in flowers—and corn stalks. Not the corn of the twentieth century, but a peculiar, eight-rowed type, small by modern standards. The rich soil, fed by the dead bodies and warmed by the sun, had yielded the ancestor of the corn that, ironically, fattened the cattle that would be slaughtered for a cheap meal.

The experts said, after months of careful digging and cataloguing, that under the corn and the tarp were three distinct, incredible archaeological finds: an altar carved out of the stone wall against which it was found, and on it a delicately carved urn in which they found traces of honey; a dolman housing the remains of a prehistoric woman, with a small leather pouch still intact around what would have been her waist and was now only bone; and a small cairn—a pile of carefully piled stones—in which a young child's skeleton, determined to be male, laid peacefully, his little hand pointing in the direction of his mother.

The urn's carving helped the archaeology team, specially called in from Trinity College, Dublin, to determine the age of the remains under the tarp; they were almost eight thousand years old. The team also unearthed a large viaduct under the rise; the theory was that originally the Mayans had harnessed the towering mountain's stream to run past the rise, providing water for their rituals as well as for the inhabitants of a village on the site. The team had amassed a great deal of knowledge about the place, even its name: it had been called Ouxacotl.

18

MLA

When the music plays, I hear the words I had to follow
Once upon a time.
Moody Blues, *Your Wildest Dreams*

Zia took out her diary and began to write: *'Dream after waking'—*
November 11th.

She put the pen down and rubbed her eyes. A look at the clock told her it was 2:06 a.m., and she sighed. It was hard enough for her to sleep when she wasn't in her own bed, but the dream she'd just had made sleep impossible.

Zia was staying with her sister, Caroline, for a few days. Caro had invited Zia to stay when she heard she was going to speak at the Midwest Language Association's convention in Chicago. Zia's presentation was called "Friar Knowledge" and included her research on Christopher Marlowe's *The Tragicall History of the Life and Death of Doctor Faustus*, focusing on how the succubus, Helen of Troy, caused Faustus' eventual damnation. Caro didn't care much for literature, but she did like having Zia stay with her, especially now that Zia was living so far away, in Portland, Oregon.

Zia adjusted her glasses, picked up her pen, and continued to write down the dream she'd had.

†

"Caroline had a house; I was staying with her in Chicago while going to the conference. Cassidy (my granddaughter) was living with her, not Kat, and Kat was nowhere to be seen. The house was adobe (mostly), all curved walls, smooth walls. Cass had her own part of the house where she was studying, and she also had some sort of a kid's show on: she could watch it from this little Easy Bake Oven kind of thing. Cass was younger than she is now, but not so young as to play with the things that were in her "room." (It was more of a large, long, many-leveled, dormer-like space, with walls of smooth light brown adobe.) She had her own little sink in an alcove, almost like a shrine.

"She was really happy to see me, but Caro had her so busy, she didn't really have any time to play with Nana Zia. Of course, I was there for a conference anyway, and I still didn't have my speech written.

"Caro was busy in the kitchen, a space I've seen before in many dreams, with the kitchen appliances all on the left, and in a sort of hall. Very light and airy toward the far end, away from where Caro was preparing some scant meal. (She's always on a diet, though she doesn't need to be.)

"I was faint from hunger and traveling, but wanted to press on because of trying to get the speech done. Caro was talking away to me, in that stern-ish, cracking-jokes-but-really-hating-life way she has, so that you slip up, agreeing with whatever "bad" situation she's talking about, and then she turns it on *you*, like you're the one who started the complaint, and you were only agreeing with her. I hate that; I think it's something I do, too. We were taught not to complain; instead, we crack jokes and make the situation funny, thinking we're hiding it. We're not, apparently, because smart people realize we've got a veiled complaint going. They agree with us to be nice, then we come down on them like a ton of bricks. Ha! It's so much easier to accuse others of having a negative attitude than to see it in myself.

"I was actually feeling so bad, though, that I could only half listen to her. I felt like I have in some of my dreams, especially the ones I have after I wake up (if you know what I mean), in which I feel drugged, and the strongest thing I've had for the past twelve hours has been tea. I was standing next to Caro's fridge, my left hand on it to steady myself, and suddenly my words were in slo-mo, and I was sinking, very slowly, to the floor. Caro was alarmed; she put the knife down that had been in her hand, and she gave me some orange juice. I remember it tasting very bitter—I never drink orange juice anymore, though I did religiously for many, many years, first thing in the morning.

"Caro suggested that I go to my room and have a lie-down. My room was in some other part of the huge house, and I went in search of it, for I had forgotten where it was. I passed Cassidy working away at her little sink and listening to instructional videos, or whatever. She smiled; always happy to see me is my little Cassers.

"I went into this adobe-clad hall, still in that same Milka chocolate bar color; smooth, cool, beautiful. Every now and then I'd have to duck as the ceilings, like either an old basement, or like old-fashioned dormers, would have an angular bit coming down, nearly taking the head off me.

"Then I came to a tiny alcove on the left, similar to the 'shrine' at which Cassidy had her sink. There were two porcelain-capped plumbing holes for where the taps should be. The sink was there, but no taps, in other words. I thought, *This might not be where Caro wants me to stay then.* As if she could hear through walls, I could hear Caro's faint voice say (for I was a long way away), 'You'll be able to wash your hands down here.'

"Around the corner from the sink (which had one of those low overhangs right before it, and one after) was a tiny staircase built into the adobe, winding to the left. I wondered what was up there, and ventured up one or two steps. There, ahead of me, at the top of the tiny stairs, I could see two headstones. Surrounding them were things like turquoise beads and semi-precious stones in a color I'd never seen before—a beautiful orange, like the sun at sunset. The headstones themselves were weathered, lichen-spotted, and there was raised lettering on them I could not read.

"The room in which the graves stood had wonderful light streaming in, striking the stones. The windows (those kind they have in adobe houses, but longer, wider, and taller) ran the length of two walls, the one on the left of where I was coming up the stairs, and the one facing me. I could see blue, blue sky, and green tree-leaves against the windows ahead of me. The headstones were placed such that one was a little taller, or seemed so, for the other, the one on the right, was leaning against it, as if the woman who had been this man's companion in life were leaning into the crook of her beloved's shoulder. It was a peaceful, beautiful, not-scary-at-all kind of place. I felt like I was witnessing something heavenly, that I had intruded on their peaceful sleep. If they woke up, I believed they would be happy to see me, smiling.

"I ventured closer to the stones. Gently, I scratched the raised part that had the names. To my surprise, the lichen fell off easily, and I could read "Tuck."

"My heart stopped beating, and I couldn't breathe. As quickly as I could, I backed down the stairs, sweating and crying. For Tuck, of course, is my very best friend in the whole world, and he is very much alive. I was afraid to see whose name was on the other, the leaning, tombstone.

"As I moved backward down the few steps, I marveled at Caro's buying a house with these graves in it. Surely she knew they were here, for I would say they were a feature of the home.

"In front of me a few steps away, through a smooth-arched doorway, was Caro's bedroom. She had a beautiful bed, the kind I would like myself. There was a crimson throw on it; it was a round bed, comfortable, different from other beds Caro has bought in the past. It was pushed up against the corner of two adobe walls. The floor was stone, and Caro had placed a beautiful woven rug, with an image of the sun in red and orange, next to the bed, on the right. There was a small chest at the foot of the bed, with blankets piled neatly on it.

"There was, along the wall with the headboard, to the right of the bed, a sort of window (no glass) cut into the wall. Walking up to it, I surmised it was a grotto, for I could see the floor was flush with the bottom part of the window through which I looked. I was in for another shock: there, in the grotto (and placed so it would have been directly behind my sister's bed) was what I can only call a shrine—apparently to a dead race car driver. There was a black leather, studded motorcycle jacket crudely tacked up against a big, heart-shaped, floral wreath. The flowers were as dead as whoever was in the grave; they had been white, but they were all tipped with rusty brown now, and looked brittle. Written in blood on a huge knife that had been placed in the center of the jacket front were the words "TRUE LUV." (My anagram-loving mind immediately transposed those letters into "VULTURE.")

"In contrast to the other grotto, this place had no light coming in, and it was much, much smaller. There were various things—car keys, a helmet, racing gloves—piled in front of the "headstone." Directly facing me was a nearly illegible, huge poster of some French heartthrob from the early 60s. The poster had seen better days.

"Two thoughts struck me in quick succession: first, How on earth can Caro sleep knowing that's behind her head? And the second: Both grottos are for people who loved each other very much. And then another thought struck me: Caro was this French guy's lover. And we never knew; none of her family ever knew.

"Still in the dream, I decided to go back downstairs and stay in a room without so many memories. Caro was very matter-of-fact, although she must have realized what I'd seen. She continued to bustle around the kitchen, and said I could stay in the 'room' downstairs near the kitchen. I went down another hall, a long one, one I hadn't seen before. This looked entirely different; business-like, in fact. No adobe here. It was like a row of offices, with window-blinded windows placed halfway down from the top of the wall and open partway, all down the hall on both sides. The rooms appeared connected from the outside, but they were actually individual rooms, compartments really, and I looked for one in which to cage myself.

"Next I found myself talking to a man—dark-haired, kind of a longish-face (but well-fed), suited (dark, white shirt, tie)—who talked to me in a kind of office *cum* library. He represented the MLA and the conference. I had gone in, I think, to tell him that I wasn't finished with my presentation. I introduced myself: 'Hi, I'm Zia—'

"'Delighted to meet you! I recognize your name, and don't worry! You'll be fine! I've read your paper already, and it's exactly what we're looking for!' (I know—most MLA-types are not prone to exclamation marks, but this one apparently was.)

"I was thinking, *there's no way he's talking about me, as I know I don't have my paper finished.* 'I think you might be confusing me with someone else. There may be another—'

"'No, really, don't be so modest,' he said, herding me across the crimson carpet and out the wood-paneled door. 'Looking forward to hearing you speak!'

"What a strange dream. . ."

†

Zia, tired of writing now, but happy she was able to get it all down, put the pen down, turned off the light, and went back to bed. She could hear Caro padding about in the hall outside her door. *She must not be able to sleep either.* As Zia snuggled into the warm bed, she heard her sister's lovely voice singing one of her favorite Irish songs:

Her eyes, they shine like the diamonds;

You'd swear she was queen of the land.

And her hair hung over her shoulders,

Tied up with a black velvet band.

19

Birthday

Time is a river, flowin' into nowhere
We will live while we can; we will have our ever after.
Steve Winwood, "Finer Things"

Tuck awoke from another bad dream. In it, he was left alone in a movie theater, or at least he thought he was alone. People kept drifting into life and out of it, seeming to appear and disappear without reason. He could see himself on a big screen, a screen like the one on the new platinum HD television his Aunt Eimear had just bought. He didn't have a TV himself, and didn't think that he'd get one, either. There was so little on television that he could watch. As a child, he would not have been allowed to watch the kinds of things in the dream he'd just had, the one that woke him in terror.

In addition to the movie theater, he dreamed he fell off a mountain. He was part of a climbing expedition—that made sense, as he loved to climb—but he dressed funny and he spoke a different language. At another point in the dream, he was a rope around a burning witch; he was a monk (doing things that made him blush even thinking about it); he was a farmer in the mountains with a beautiful wife; he might have been an animal (his mouth still kind of tasted like grass); and at another point, he was a race car driver who had crashed. The violence of the image—a wall of flame twenty feet high coming at him—caused him to wake up, screaming.

Zia rushed into the room, running to his bedside and cradling his sweating body against her own. "My god, Tuck, what's the matter? Did you have a bad dream?" She held him away from her slightly, feeling his forehead with the back of her hand. "It doesn't feel like you've got a fever, at least." She pointed toward the brightly curtained window. "See how light it is outside? I wondered why you were sleeping so late. The morning's half gone already." She got up from the bed, went over to the window, opened the curtains wide, and lifted the sash. Cool September air rushed in, and Tuck felt better instantly. "Then again," she continued, "it *is* your birthday—September 8th. You're entitled to sleep in if you want." She sat back down on the edge of the bed, near Tuck. "Do you want to tell me about the nightmare?"

Tuck nodded, then began to recount the entire dream to her, respectfully leaving out the embarrassing parts, prefacing the story by saying, "It's not exactly a nightmare, because there were wonderful parts in it, really beautiful parts. And funny parts, too." Zia nodded as he told her this, thoughtfully.

Then, when he was only partway through his story—the part where he thought he was a goat, she laid her right hand on his left, the hand that was above the bedclothes. "And something bad happened to the woman, didn't it?" Her eyes misted over. "I know what happens next, Tuck."

Stunned, Tuck didn't know what to say at first. Then, tentatively, as though feeling his way through a dark tunnel toward a faint light, he said, "You've had the same dream, haven't you?"

"Yes," she said, simply. "And I'll bet you thought you were dead several times, too." Tuck nodded, slowly, mesmerized. Zia continued, "Seriously, I can tell you that you were not dreaming, and you didn't die. And I'm not certain myself how it really happens, but things—and people—don't appear from nowhere. They're here all the time, it's just that we don't see them until we need them, or ask for them in some way." She held both his hands, excited now. "Do you remember sitting in the theater, with each of your beer bottles in one of the cup holders? And you rolling that joint?" She giggled. "I was behind you in the theater the whole time, but you didn't expect to see me, so you didn't. In what I thought was *my* dream, I was hired by the people who owned the place, to write—or record, really—a sort of history of those who are here at any given time. I was supposed to sit in the last row and just take notes and make observations, trying not to judge. I had no idea you'd arrive, but I'm glad you did—even if you didn't notice me for ages." She smiled and said, "Which life did you like best?"

"Wait a second," said Tuck, puzzled. "You're saying I actually did all those things? lived those lives?" He scratched his head. His face lit up. "You mean I actually won an Olympic gold medal? Two of them? In Saint-Moritz? Cool." He smiled broadly, "This is the best present ever!" He shuddered slightly. "I'm glad I'm not dead any more," he said, remembering the wall of flame.

"But wait," he said, the puzzled look returning. "Why do I find myself in the middle of a crisis—usually—when I realize I'm in a different body?"

"Because, my dear Tuck, crises give us true glimpses of ourselves; at least, that's been my experience. It takes each of us a certain amount of time to realize who we are; why we're here. People arrive in our lives when we need them. Every single person in the story is someone you need at that time, but not only that: every person you meet, as Carl Jung said about the figures in our dreams, is a facet of *you*. That's the scary part, isn't it?" Zia could see the look of concentration on Tuck's face.

"But everything seems so real! It doesn't seem like a dream at all—"

"That's because it isn't, Tuck."

"You're saying all these things really happened to me..."

"Yes." She smoothed her multi-colored, swishy, long skirt over her—he could tell because they stuck out a little—knobby-ish knees. "Like I said before, it's all real."

"Promise?"

"Yupper-doodles." She giggled. "Like Steve Martin says in *Three Amigos*, 'It's real!'"

"What about the time differences though?" Tuck persisted. There doesn't seem to be any rhyme or reason to what happens." He shook his head, perplexed. "Sometimes I know should still be alive somewhere, but I'm in two places at the same time. I think I'm in the present; then I'm on a 1950s hiking expedition; then I seem to be in some medieval place... I mean, really, Zia, what's up with all that?"

"I think time is something humans made up so they could feel they had control over something in their crazy world. The same qualities that separate us from other animals—being able to plan, hypothesize, dream, for example—also bring the need to compartmentalize, to order time in some way so we feel our planning, hypothesizing, and dreaming will make sense." She laughed, that deep throaty chuckle of delight that Tuck so loved. "And since the English Renaissance, and especially after the Enlightenment, white men—colonialists and capitalists—have been all about making sense, being 'rational,' as they felt only white men like themselves could be. They ignored the thousands of years of previous history that pointed to there being very little rhyme or reason, if any, to what went on here on Earth."

She leaned forward, serious now. "What you've been experiencing; what I, too, experience; *is* the norm, as far as the universe goes. Someone said—Ruth Rendell's Inspector Wexford, maybe—that time is like a big puddle that we find ourselves walking in—does it matter which way it sloshes? Or which way we walk in or through it? Is there only one right way?" She paused, sitting back in the big wicker chair with the soft green cushions. "Changing our concept of time, seeing it as more fluid, would help explain why everyone experiences life in a different way, and why we feel sometimes like we've been there already." She smiled again. "I believe we happen to have walked into that puddle together, holding hands, and have never let go."

She stretched her hand out then to him, catching his small, strong brown hand in her own. "Come on, son. Let's see if there's any popcorn left. We'll make some, okay? She looked down at her Tuck, squeezing his hand.

"And can you put lots of real butter on it, mom?" Tuck rubbed his stomach, rolling his eyes in delight. "You *know* how much I love butter."

20

Mezzanine

All of us are in the gutter,
but some of us are looking at the stars.
Oscar Wilde

Tuck found himself walking down a deep-red-carpeted hall, one that curved gently, irrevocably, to his left. There were imitation Victorian sconces on the wall, the kind that—had they truly been Victorian—would have held candles, not the light bulbs that look like tapered candles that were in each of them now. Tuck noticed that a few of them had burned out; no one had bothered to replace them. There were no doors to either side of him; the ceiling, off-white, was coved and had plaster work that belied the tackiness of the hall's other furnishings. For one thing, the walls were papered in that god-awful, crimson-flocked wallpaper that could be found in cheap hotels and Legion halls when he was growing up. *Which time?* he thought, a wry expression crossing his face. *It's like that paper in the old Rivoli theater. Wonder if that's still around.*

Tuck stopped dead in his tracks. He looked carefully around him, and up, and down. He closed his eyes; then he took a slow, deliberate lungful of air, through his nostrils, feeling it as it passed the openings and traveled down into his lungs.

Popcorn. With fresh butter—real butter. He sniffed again, just to make sure. *Yes, that's it, all right. Popcorn, just like I remember it. I'm in the Rivoli. But when? This just doesn't look familiar.* His eyes took in the hallway, the frescoed ceiling, the cheesy wallpaper, the fake sconces, the red carpet that belonged in a bordello. He decided to keep walking and see what happened. He followed the curved hallway for maybe two or three minutes at most, walking slowly and looking for clues to the year he might be in.

Then, to his left, a long balcony—a mezzanine, really—opened to his view. A beautiful balustrade, decorated to complement the frescoed ceiling of the hallway, swept majestically in a semi-circle. Tuck walked over to the balustrade and looked down.

There it all was: The refreshment stand, located straight in front of him, only a floor down; the entrance to the actual viewing room, visible on his right; to the left, the hallway to the bathrooms was laid out, just as he remembered it, except at a distance, a different perspective. There was Toothy, or someone very like him, asking people if they wanted *fum* Diet Coke. He could hear very well up here; the voices traveled so it sounded like the people were addressing him, Tuck. There were people waiting in line for treats; he could see people at the ticket counter, way in back, hoping to get in; there were people filing in to watch the feature film.

Tuck remembered to look up, and what he saw astounded him. "This place goes right up! Look at that! Why, it's a rotunda kind of thing!" he marveled out loud. *There was one similar to this, only smaller, inside the theater. It seemed to recede every time I got close to it.* The one he looked at now was stunning, the colors true—not faded like the one he'd seen before. The Wheel of Fortune was done in brilliant blues, golds, oranges, and reds. The figure of Fortuna looked almost human in her regal finery; the figure still caught on the wheel had an agonized look that touched Tuck's heart. *I never noticed this before, when I came to the Rivoli. And it was here all the time, I'll bet.* He had a sudden thought. *What if...?* He looked over the balustrade.

Not a soul was in sight. Toothy; the ticket buyers; the ticket sellers; the moviegoers; they were all gone. *No. Not again.* But this time he was in a different position. Maybe he could do something now that he couldn't do before.

From the left, from the hallway on the left where the bathrooms were, a movement caught his eye. A mincing figure, wearing impossibly high heels—stilettos—walked into the hall, *mmm*ing her lips with their fresh coating of red lipstick. She dimpled briefly in the foyer's mirrored wall, snapped her leather clutch shut, tucked it under her trim arm, and looked around. Tuck could see the panic rise in her eyes as she realized no one was there—no one at all. She started back to the bathrooms, but the hallway had vanished. She had no idea what to do. Her first thought must have been to call someone, for she snapped open the Gucci purse to get her phone. No phone.

Tuck couldn't bear to watch any more. "Look up!' he cried, tears streaming down his face. "For god's sake, look up, Zia!"

†

Zia sensed, rather than heard, the voice that called her name. It sounded like it came from above, so that's where she looked—up. All she could see were screens; eight screens, like big plasma TVs, hanging in a circle around the foyer.

EPILOGUE

Your stairway lies on the whispering wind.
Led Zeppelin, "Stairway to Heaven"

They were the only two on the beach, a narrow, long stretch of sand, with the curve of the quay maybe a mile ahead of them. All along the beach stretched the detritus of seaweed and kelp, left by the receding tide, to be swept back out to sea when the tide returned.

It was early September, the eighth. The sky was a glorious blue and dotted with fluffy clouds; the wind held no hint of the chill that would soon blow over the island. The woman wore a white gauzy outfit, the wide-legged trousers rolled up on her shapely calves so she could, barefooted, walk the damp shore. The man wore similar clothing, white and gauzy, and he, too, had the trouser legs rolled up so they wouldn't get wet. The two of them laughed a lot, picking their way over the bulbous kelp and splashing through the tide pools teeming with tiny marine life.

They stood still for a moment, gazing out at the green, choppy sea, holding hands and smiling—for a moment at each other, then out at the glorious landscape, almost lunar, before them. A piece of kelp, caught by the wind, whipped lightly against the left calf of the lovely woman. She bent down to see what had touched her, swooping her long, dark hair away from her eyes as she leaned down.

"Oh, look!" she said to her companion. "Look at this exquisite shell!" At her feet, millimeters from her left little toe, was a beautiful shell. "And I nearly stepped on it! Let's take it home with us." She picked it up, cradling it in her left hand and stroking it with her right. They both peered at it, up close.

"Is there anything inside?" asked the man.

"No, I don't think so." She shook it, and some grains of sand tumbled out. "No, just sand." She smiled. "But I'll bet something lived in there before! I wonder what happened to the poor thing." She put the shell in her pocket and the two of them continued their walk down the beach.

†

And with those small gestures, a moment in a careless hand, Tuck's and Zia's world ended, just grains of sand on an endless beach.

About the Author

✝

Jennifer Holland was born in Crystal, Minnesota and raised in Onalaska, Wisconsin. She has also lived in Utah, Idaho, Washington, California, and Oregon, as well as having lived nearly twelve years in Ireland. Her employment has been as varied as Tuck's life: she has been an ESL teacher, a student, a journalist, an amateur actress and singer, and a secretary, to name a few. These experiences have contributed to her stories, as well as her longtime fascination with sex, death, and the meaning of life.

A published poet and scholar, Director's Cut *is her first novel. Two further novels are in the pipeline:* MarginAlias, *on Portland's homeless, and* Death Keeps Barging In, *one that answers the burning question, "Can my dead mom see what I'm doing right now?" A non-fiction book on virginity in seventeenth century literature (particularly works by Margaret Cavendish) is also in progress.*

Currently she is in a publishing master's program at Portland State University in Portland, Oregon.

Acknowledgements

✝

I want to thank Don Warnke for his editing assistance; Susan Hanley for her humor and vision; the authors and editors Karen Kirtley and Vinnie Kinsella for their invaluable advice (and providing the original impetus for entering the 2008 NaNoWriMo contest, for which I wrote Director's Cut*); my dear Libyan and Saudi friends for not only assuring the verity of the "Sand" chapter, but cheering me on; and my children, friends, and family for their unflagging belief in my ability to write. I need to thank Wikipedia and Encyclopedia Britannica (online versions) for the information on Henri Oreiller, the history of ale, and the inspiration for the K2 section. Thank you, too, to the M/MLA, who really did accept the paper on Marlowe's Faustus I presented in November 2008 in Minneapolis. The snippets of music are from some of my favorite songs; I see Sting's "A Thousand Years" as the theme song if* Director's Cut *ever becomes a movie.*

The rest, I'm afraid, is purely fictional.